Death Takes
Center Stage

Death Takes Center Stage

Elizabeth Ireland

BOOKLOGIX®

Alpharetta, Georgia

ISBN: 978-1-61005-328-0
Library of Congress Control Number: 2013905341

Printed in the United States of America

∞This paper meets the requirements of ANSI/NISO Z39.48-1992 (Permanence of Paper)

This is a work of fiction. Names, characters, places, and incidents are either the product of the author's imagination or are used fictitiously. Any resemblance to actual persons living or dead is entirely coincidental. While some events depicted are historical fact, the author's treatment of them is entirely fictional.

Cover Art: Julie Grace, Grace Design
www.gracedesign.net

www.ElizabethIreland.net
www.BackstageMystery.com

For Paula Keenan,
best BFF ever

*Forgiveness is the fragrance that the violet
sheds on the heel that has crushed it.*
— Mark Twain

To beguile the time,
Look like the time; bear welcome in your eye,
Your hand, your tongue: look like the innocent flower,
But be the serpent under't.

Macbeth Act I, Scene 5

~~~~~~

PROLOGUE

Irene Davenport despised Chicago. It was the city in which, through supreme force of will, and not a little talent, she had begun her career as an actress. It was far too closely connected to the persona she had left behind her and the man who had propelled her into a life in the theater. The man with the coldest of hearts, Roger Plant. It had been winter when she had made her debut in the city, performing a walk-on role as a maid in a comedy, the title of which even she had forgotten. Now, twenty years later, in the sweltering fall of 1871, she found herself right back where she had begun her career. Only this time, she was the major attraction.

She had been charmed by Augustin Daly, as she always was. Of course, she had her own reasons for being here at this time, and Daly's offer was just too much to resist—star of a new combination company, a promise that the production would tour for a year and a comfortable, secure salary of three thousand a week. On top of all that, the Chicago run included an all-expense paid suite at the Sherman House. How could she refuse? She had always made her own rules, and this first stop on the tour would be no exception. The money alone went a long way to making her forget how much she disliked being back in Chicago.

All this she considered as she sat in her private dressing room, in between scenes, and contemplated her reflection in the make-up mirror.

Those who met her in person were surprised at how small and how delicate she was. She appeared much taller, bigger, and full of life on stage. Part of this was her projection and part of it was arranged artifice on her behalf. Onstage, she cleverly managed to maneuver herself onto a step or a platform so that she would appear slightly taller than, or at least equal in height to, her leading men. She always arranged for her male counterpart to be no more than half an inch taller than her five-foot-two frame.

This was one of her many personal vanities. However, it did not detract from her performance. Irene Davenport never disappointed an audience. She was, when all was said and done, a monumental talent. Incomparable as Lady Macbeth, she wore a costume hand-made to her specific design: a dress molded to her exquisite figure, the subdued bustle was the height of current fashion. As if woven with moonbeams, the dark shimmering fabric caught whatever light was available and held it, enhancing her personal charisma. In tribute to the play, a tartan shawl was added to her costume. It was artfully arranged on top of her right shoulder, draped across her back and under her left arm, then brought up the front of her chest and fastened with a large, intricate Celtic pin on top of her right shoulder.

Beads of perspiration collected at her hairline and she impatiently brushed them away. Ordinarily, by the end of September, cooling breezes blew off Lake Michigan and refreshed the city air, but not this year. She had read in the *Chicago Journal* that there had been no rainfall to speak of this past summer. The night before, there had been a fire— apparently a common event during the past few months. However that did not deter the audience this evening. Even though the air was so still, so stifling, that every lady who had the foresight to bring a fan was making prodigious use of it, not a seat in the 2,600-capacity theater was empty. Instead, there was an aura of excited expectation. Irene felt it, savored it, loved it. Now they were waiting for her last entrance.

This reminded her how disappointed she was in this, the opening night performance. She simply did not comprehend what was going on. Strange mistakes were being made, props were misplaced and cues were off. There had been a problem with the downstage trap doors and the appearance of the three witches had been late. The elevator mechanism ran unevenly lending the emergence of the witches an almost laughable quality. She felt she had to make up for it and was giving a tour de force performance of what was already an illustrious career. Lady Macbeth was her favorite role; she adored playing it and loved the way the audience worshipped her in response. But tonight, everything that could possibly go wrong had. She blamed a good part of it on the actor who portrayed Macbeth, Edward Hearne. *What a poor excuse for a man*, she thought to herself. She had no idea how he fancied himself a leading man. If he was not drunk now, she knew he very soon would be. Everyone knew that he kept a "water" pitcher on the prop table and poured himself a glass before entering or leaving the stage. In their scenes together, she could smell the scent of alcohol on his breath. The last rehearsal had been decent. She simply could not understand why things were now going so poorly!

A trickle of sweat coursed down her lovely spine, but she disregarded it. She stared at the reflection in the mirror. Her thoughts shifted to her own appearance. What she saw pleased her—black hair, deep green eyes, a heart-shaped face with a completely clear, porcelain complexion. She was small in stature, but her figure was perfect. A "pocket Venus." She exuded a presence that simply could not be ignored. If she chose, she could make her every move— whether an entrance onto a stage or into a restaurant— draw the attention of every person present.

Her reverie was interrupted by the arrival of her personal dresser, the crane-like Beatrice O'Neill, almost fifty, thin to the point of emaciation, and dressed immaculately in black. She carried a jewelry case.

"I brought the pearls, Mrs. Davenport."

The title was honorary, for Irene had yet to marry. Nevertheless, she was well aware that as a woman in the theater, one had to have the title in order to garner some respect from the outside world. It was all part of the mystique she had created about herself.

Irene glanced up at the willowy matron who also functioned as her personal assistant. Beatrice had proven herself invaluable many times, and the actress knew how much Beatrice adored her. She would miss Beatrice's attention in the new life she was contemplating for herself. For now, she merely nodded, and her aide opened the case, lovingly removed the pearls, and handed them to Irene. They were Irene's trademark—a rope of flawlessly matched Orientals, rumored to have cost a fortune and presented to her by a grateful lover. Only Irene knew that story was a myth, having invented it herself. In reality, the baubles were paste. An extremely expensive and authentic-looking paste, but counterfeit all the same.

She carefully placed them around her neck. They hung below her waist and were knotted close to the end. She always wore them as part of her costume, regardless of what role she performed.

O'Neill silently backed away to put the case in the travelling trunk. Once more, Irene brought her attention back to the mirror. Her expression hardened as she thought about those waiting for her on stage.

She was interrupted by an abrupt knock on her dressing room door. Bobby Martin poked his head in. The gangly thirteen-year-old call boy got on her nerves, so before he could even say, "Places, Mrs. Davenport," she screamed "Get out!" He disappeared without a word.

She took a deep breath and stood up. She smoothed back her flawless hair, checked her make-up and found nothing out of place and everything to be perfect. She adjusted the long strand of signature pearls and smiled. Touching her pearls always calmed her down, made her feel more at ease. She went through the door, down a hallway, up a winding stairway and out onto the dimly lit backstage area. Her countenance was a careful mask, which she had thoughtfully arranged in preparation for her next scene. Not now, not ever, did she let her face betray any personal sensibility. However, her deep, green eyes flashed with dangerous emotion and there was an almost electric energy about her that warned all who approached to keep their distance.

Out of the corner of her eye, she saw Edward and ignored him. She walked past Mary Cosgrove, one of the young women hired from among local actors, and pointedly ignored her as well. She looked around and wondered where the other one was—Lily or Lottie, something like that—the giddy girl who played the Gentlewoman and introduced her next scene. Irene spotted her...on the wrong side of the stage. *Where is Teddy? He's the stage manager, so why isn't he watching that girl*, she hissed to herself. The *entr'acte* was almost over and Irene impatiently waited for the performance of Harold Jordan, the tall and gawky tenor who was singing an insipid love song, to come to its tedious conclusion.

She took a deep breath and waited. *Where is that boy?* In the next instant, Bobby rushed over to her with a single, white candle in his hand. She reached over and grabbed it from him.

"Light it, you fool," she hissed at him.

His hand shaking, Bobby struck the match several times before it finally sparked and the wick flickered and caught. He quickly backed off and disappeared.

Irene heard the polite applause from the audience as Jordan quickly took his bow in front of the act curtain and stepped through the slit where it joined. He was about to exit stage left when he saw Irene standing there. Wisely, he chose the opposite side of the stage, even though it meant he had to dodge around some scenery that was set for her scene. He pitied anybody who had to go near Irene just now.

The audience quickly settled down into a restless hum of incoherent comments and chatter. With the change of music, a sense of expectancy settled over the house. It was time for Lady Macbeth's final appearance and each patron sat up a little straighter and leaned forward. The girl who had been on the wrong side of the stage made a dash for the correct side and ran directly behind Irene as quickly as she could. Irene was outraged, but before she could take the stupid girl to task, the act curtain slowly rolled back, the well-oiled pulleys making almost no sound as the heavy, deep blue velvet material parted and opened to reveal the courtyard of Macbeth's castle.

The Doctor and the Gentlewomen moved onstage. Irene waited and listened. The actors began their speeches.

Irene straightened her shoulders and moved gracefully toward the center of the stage. She stepped onto the platform specifically placed for her to increase her height over the other actors and force them to turn their backs to the audience and look at her. Out of the corner of her right eye, she could see several people, including the disgusting drunk, Edward Hearne, cue up for the next scene. *Let him watch. Perhaps he would learn something about acting!*

To the audience, it was if she had suddenly appeared, emerging like a phantom from the darkness. There was no applause, just the combined, sudden intake of breath in twenty-six hundred throats. Applause was beyond them. In that one incandescent moment, every man wanted her and every woman wanted to be her.

Only the faint hiss of the gas lamps could be heard as she slowly turned her body, taking her time. As she raised her head, the unearthly light from the candle illuminated her face and sent eerie shadows dancing across the stage floor. Her expression revealed a woman whose sanity was completely gone, a woman caught in fear and guilt from committing an act of murder, a woman without peace or solace, not even in sleep. She began to move and then, suddenly stopped. Her eyes wide open, she faced the audience, but did not focus on them. In that moment, Irene completely felt her power and knew that this was a role she absolutely owned, that she was the Lady Macbeth of her generation.

As the light slowly came up behind her, the walls of the castle were revealed, yet cast in shadow. She waited for one of the Gentlewomen to say her line. And then her moment came.

"Yet, here's a spot," she whispered.

Her perfectly modulated, perfectly tuned voice—the product of years of intensive training and use—effortlessly projected to every seat in the theater and commanded each ear to listen. She wove her magic upon them, forced them to bear witness to the crumbling mind of a woman who, through relentless ambition, had pushed her husband to regicide. She was a woman in despair and fear of the penance she must now face for the execution of a most grievous murder, a woman out of touch with all reality. She cried out:

"Here's the smell of the blood still; All the perfumes of Arabia will not sweeten this little hand. Oh! Oh! Oh!"

As she slowly worked her way across the stage, she became a woman possessed by her own insanity.

Irene did not wander all over the stage as many who played this role often did. Instead, she swayed slightly, seemingly caught in the throes of the consequences of her character's actions. The audience was swept away by the pain of her experience and many were moved to tears by her actions now. She worked her way to her last speech, not in extreme emotion, but by pulling that emotion from the audience themselves. All too soon, she came to her last speech. Tearless, but vibrating with the resultant pain of her actions, she moaned:

"To bed, to bed: there's knocking at the gate. Come, come, come, come, give me your hand.

What's done cannot be undone. To bed, to bed, to bed."

She blew out the candle and, phantom-like, floated off the stage. There was a moment of silence. Just as one of the Gentlewomen was about to speak, twenty-six hundred pairs of hands came together to form their tribute. The applause was overwhelming, incredible. It became a wave that grew stronger and stronger. When Irene stepped out from the wings, their voices added to their praise. The stifling heat was forgotten; in that moment, they simply expressed their adoration of the Great Davenport.

She merely stood. After a moment of absorbing the applause, she went to the center of the stage. The extraneous actors left. They knew their speeches would go unheard anyway and they quickly backed into the wings and off the stage, leaving Irene alone.

In the house, the audience was on its feet. The ovation became louder, stronger, overwhelming. Irene smiled. Exhilarated, vindicated, she gracefully took a step forward and made her deep actor's bow to them, those luminous pearls just kissing the oak planks of the stage floor. She felt wonderful. She raised her arms and spread them out to encompass the entire theater. Her face was a mirror of their adoration, gratefully accepted.

Bobby Martin trotted across the stage, almost completely hidden behind the huge bouquet of thirty-six long stemmed golden roses. A startled look of annoyance flickered across her face, as she wondered who would have thought to send her yellow roses. She noticed a card, and the thought occurred to her that this must be some trick played upon her by her co-star. She arranged her face into a beatific smile and bowed to accept them, gently rubbing her cheek against the delicate yellow blooms. Bobby darted off the stage.

She looked up straight into the faces of her audience and allowed a single tear to course down her right cheek, her best side. She took several slow, dancer-like steps backward, her arms a mass of yellow blooms.

Behind her, the scenery began to change for the next scene, which took place in the forest of Birnam Wood. Her anger returned in a flash. She wondered, with an internal scowl, who dared take focus away from her in this moment. The applause started to slacken, but Irene did not leave the stage. The main curtain began to close. Taking one final deep bow, she lowered her head almost to the floor and then threw it back in a triumph-filled gesture. Her pearls, following the momentum of that effort, swung back behind her and caught on the scenery. The applause picked up one final time and she decided that now was the moment to leave.

She turned, but, as if caught by an invisible hand, she was yanked back. The scenery moved upwards and was lifted into the fly space. Irene was caught and pulled backwards. The knot in her pearls slipped toward her head and began to tighten around her throat. She felt herself being slowly pulled upward. The pearls dug into her neck and she felt the pressure of each one against her delicate skin.

At first, she was merely surprised and startled. *What new disaster is this?* she asked herself. She put her right hand up to her neck and tried to loosen the pearls, which only drew tighter. All pretenses were then cast aside; she panicked and dropped the roses, as both of her hands reached up to grab the white, translucent noose around her neck. The roses hit the floor, sending several yellow petals floating up and then gently back down to the stage, where they softly landed, abandoned on the scarred floor.

The orchestra, which had been playing background music, stopped abruptly. The applause completely died out, replaced by confusion. The audience watched as Irene's feet rose from the stage floor, and still the scenery continued to move up and into the fly space. She pulled at her pearls. In blind terror now, she concentrated only on wrenching away the pearls, but was ineffective against the ever-tightening noose. Her face lost its actor's mask and now showed only raw fear. As she struggled and gasped for breath, the audience finally began to comprehend what was taking place. A woman screamed in horror and that was the signal for the entire audience to merge into the aisles in an attempt to exit wherever possible.

Several men in black evening dress jumped up from the orchestra section and clambered onto the stage, dust and dirt smearing their clothes. They reached for her, but now she was just above them. They looked up into the black abyss and stood helplessly as her feet twisted and beat against the scenery.

There were shouts from backstage, but the scenery still rose. The commanding voice of Teddy Ryan yelled, "Cut the rope! Cut the damn rope, for the love of God, cut the rope!"

Almost immediately, the backdrop fell and, with it, came the body of Irene Davenport.

More screams were heard as she crashed to the stage floor with an awful sound. Her pearls broke and scattered, jumping and rolling across the stage. One came to rest near the golden petals of a rose.

The Act Curtain finally closed, shutting off the scene. In the house, all was chaos. In a sudden rush to leave the theater, the aisles became crowded rivers of elegantly dressed men and women.

On the other side of the curtain, on the stage, the men who had tried to save her formed a circle around her inert form. Her face no longer resembled the goddess they worshipped such a short time ago. Now, her eyes bulged out, her lips were hideously drawn back and her neck was red and raw where the pearls had trespassed. An aura of despair softly descended upon this small gathering, as the full impact of the disaster became reality. Irene Davenport, the greatest Lady Macbeth of her generation, was dead.

Irene Davenport felt nothing; she merely floated in a void of complete darkness. Very slowly, she became conscious of the feeling of weightlessness. Then, a curious sensation flashed through her being—a bone numbing chill that sent a whiplash of cold right through her very core. It took her breath away and threw her into a spasm of memory.

She was back on the farm where she grew up in western Illinois. It was winter and the snow was piled up to the roof of the barn. She was seven years old and had been sent out to collect wood. She was freezing. Her skin was dry and chafed and her extremities were numb. She felt as if she would never be warm again. And she was so tired; she just wanted to go to sleep. But, she knew she would be punished if she did not return with the wood and she was afraid. It was the fear that pushed her forward, the fear of what they would do to her, how they would hurt her and she could not bear it.

Then, she was back in the present, but the fear remained and expanded. Irene struggled to master it. That childhood memory was buried deep within her brain and no one knew of it. The poor, unloved childhood of Margie Conklin did not exist. It resided in the recesses of her most private thoughts. Very few people knew about Margie Conklin and certainly no one from her theatrical life. Only the myth of the talented and precocious childhood of Irene Davenport existed. A girl nothing like Margie Conklin. Irene Davenport was worshiped, adored, rich and famous. For all intents and purposes, Margie Conklin never existed.

Irene took a deep breath and exhaled slowly. It seemed to release the memory and the fear. Her breath condensed in front of her face. Why was the air so frigid? Why this sudden memory of her childhood? The feeling of the cold dissipated, but the cold itself remained. The nothingness returned.

What happened to her? A moment ago, it was so hot in the theater.

Damn this heavy costume and the gaslights and their annoying hiss.

But, she could no longer hear the hiss. There was no sound at all. There was no sense of the weight of her costume. The cold wrapped around her once again and she reached down to pull up her tartan shawl and surround herself in its warmth. It did not help.

Where had the heat gone, she wondered.

For the first time, she looked down at her hand and at her body and realized she was floating along the ceiling of the theater. She screamed. Panic flooded through her mind and her body. The visceral need to get back on to the stage floor overwhelmed her. She attempted to move in the direction, but nothing happened.

"I must get to the floor of the stage," she said, in desperation.

And immediately, she floated downward, closer and closer to the proscenium of the stage.

She looked out into the audience and was surprised to see no one there. The house was completely empty. But, it had been filled to capacity just a moment ago. She was sure of it. Once again, she thought about moving upstage and immediately found herself there. She turned to move left and downstage and nothing happened, but when she thought about moving left and down, she moved in that direction. That was when she became aware of a group of men in evening dress standing on the stage. They appeared to be looking at something or at someone on the floor in the center of the stage.

What are they doing down there? she wondered and immediately drifted toward them.

"I am here! Can't you see me?" she called out.

There was no response.

She reached out her right hand and touched the shoulder of a distinguished looking man in expensive evening clothes who was bent over the inert form on the stage. While she could see the fine texture of the cloth, she could not feel it. He shuddered and quickly looked behind him. Irene recognized him then—it was Samuel Connelly. She felt a certain power run through her. He was absolutely devoted to her. He was part of her carefully orchestrated plan for her future, for she knew he could not deny her, that he would help her.

"Samuel. I'm here. Look at me!"

Irene was right next to him, but he did not acknowledge her. His face was pale and lined with anguish. Then, she noticed his companion, a younger man, dressed just as elegantly. She recognized him as Samuel's assistant, Paul Coopersmith. The younger man reached out and gently grabbed Samuel's arm and whispered in his ear.

"I am afraid she is dead, sir. We are of no use here. We must leave before the authorities arrive."

Samuel stood up. He slowly straightened his shoulders and nodded to his companion.

"You're right, Paul. We'd best leave now," he said.

Paul nodded and took a step back, waiting for Samuel to move ahead of him. Just as he turned to go, Samuel bent down and picked something up off of the floor. It was one of her pearls. He held it in the palm of his hand for a moment and then, wrapped his fingers around it and placed it in his jacket pocket. Abruptly, he turned, nodded his head at Paul and strode from the stage. Down the steps he went and out through the empty audience, moving so quickly that the younger man had to work to keep up with him.

Furious, Irene called after him, but he did not hear her. She thought of her pearls.

"I am wearing my pearls, am I not?" she asked aloud.

She was not sure. She was not sure of anything anymore. Quickly, she looked down at her clothes and saw her pearls.

"Yes. They are here. But, how is it possible that they are also scattered across the floor?"

She began to float again and panic coursed through her. She could not control the direction in which she went nor the movement itself. Fear overwhelmed her.

"Help me!" she screamed.

She grabbed at the scenery, pulled at the side curtains trying with all her might to stop from going up and up. And then, suddenly, she stopped. The voices of the people below her came to her in murmurs overlapping one another.

"Tragic."

"Such a loss."

"What shall we do?"

"Should we move her?"

"Don't touch her."

"How could this happen?"

"Horrible, horrible."

Curiosity enveloped her as she thought about what they were saying. Once again, she glided downward.

There was a woman lying in the center of the stage floor, her body splayed at an odd angle.

Who is this, she wondered.

"Poor, poor Irene."

Her mouth hung slack as she realized that the body on the floor was her own.

How can this be? I'm here, I'm right here! I'm alive!

Drawn downward, she felt a compelling urge to return to her body. She was possessed by the need to get back into that body. She needed to be *in* that body.

Yes, yes, yes, she moaned as she made her way towards the floor.

She was close, so very close. Everywhere, there were people, people walking, staring and standing over her body, in her way. She clawed and scratched her way closer to the floor and attempted to force her way back into the body, but nothing happened. Frantically, she looked around for help, but was completely ignored. No one *saw* her. She screamed, but once again, only she heard it.

"Why can't you see me? I'm right here!"

Hovering just above her body, she looked down at the face—her face. It was horribly contorted and there was a deep, red gash across her throat. Immediately, she placed her right hand on her neck. She felt no gash. A cold streak of fear gripped her, deeper and stronger than any cold she had ever experienced.

She remembered now. The pain, the choking, the gasping for breath. Her throat, the inability to breathe. The pain, the pain...and then nothing. She took a deep breath. Was she breathing now? She felt no pain. She knew she put her foot right through that backdrop, yet her foot felt no pain.

Am I...dead? she asked herself.

She moved closer in and, once again, tried to force herself into her body. It was impossible; she no longer had any connection with her former body. She had no substance; she was merely thought now. It was as if only her mind survived. And her thoughts were what allowed her to function at all.

"Unimaginable!" she whispered.

She floated away once more. There was no longer any urgency to get back to her body. It was an ugly thing to her.

An overwhelming rage suddenly gripped her. White-hot anger coursed through her being. This was not an accident.

Who did this to me? she demanded.

Whoever it was, she would find him and she would find a way to make him pay.

A light began to shine somewhere below her and to her left. She studied it and she began to think about how beautiful it was. She found herself floating toward it. It seemed to offer warmth. There was movement in the light and it called to her. Compelled to follow it, she floated toward one of the actors. It was that new girl, but the thought of her name failed Irene.

Louise, she thought. *No. Lily? No, Lillian! Yes, that was it!*

Lillian was one of the supernumeraries hired for the production and one of the Gentlewomen who had appeared just before her sleepwalking scene.

Irene watched as Lillian was led away from the stage by Edward Hearne. It was just like that no-talent-drunk to thwart Irene at this moment. The light, though—it seemed to encircle Lillian, seemed to pulsate around her, as if it were emanating *from* her. Sparks shot out from her and sparkled like snowflakes against the sun, and then faded away. Irene was entranced. She searched the rest of people on the crowded stage. No one else had that special light. She watched as Edward sat Lillian down near the property table and handed her a glass of water. Lillian looked up at him, smiled and thanked him.

As a moth to a flame, Irene was drawn to Lillian. She moved closer and closer. Convinced now that there was some warmth there, some solace, and that she very desperately needed to be close to it, Irene moved toward Lillian and that light. No one noticed her and no one saw her. She had to get to Lillian. She had to see what that light was. She moved closer and closer until finally she was just above Lillian and she reached her hand out toward the girl.

Suddenly, she heard a voice.

"Stop!"

The sound of it reverberated through her skull and the noise became almost unbearable. Someone saw her! She turned around to try and find the person who had spoken that one clear and concise word. What she saw was a rather ordinary man in his late forties, slender, dressed not in evening wear, but work clothes. It was Teddy Ryan, the stage manager.

Is it possible, she said to herself. *Can he see me?*

He looked in her direction, but not specifically at her. She moved to her left and his eyes did not follow her. She sighed. There was no special light emanating from him. No one paid him any attention and it was obvious to her that no one else heard what he said. He stood near the stage right entrance, alone.

She suddenly remembered that Teddy was highly superstitious, obsessed with good and bad luck and knowledgeable of every myth and fable about the theater. Never having given him any serious attention before, she now regarded him with curiosity and willed herself to move closer to him.

He took a step back, apparently sensing her presence. He continued to stare, not at the rest of the people, not at the body on the stage, but up and over at her.

He sees me! He knows I'm here. Maybe he can help me.

He would help her; she would make him. At that moment, she finally noticed the expression on his face. Teddy was not happy that she was there.

He turned away from her. He walked over to Lillian, where she sat by the prop table, abandoned by Hearne. Teddy reached out and took Lillian by the elbow and led her off the stage and down to the dressing rooms. The light dissipated and faded out.

Irene felt herself move back and up into the fly space and the events taking place upon the stage faded and telescoped, moving a long way away from her.

There, she hovered, consumed in her fury. The desire for revenge flooded through her and she knew that she would have to bide her time until the right opportunity came along.

Come what come may,
Time and the hour runs through the roughest day.

Macbeth Act I, Scene 3

~~~~~~

CHAPTER ONE

It is incomprehensible to me that eighty years have passed since the night in which the great Irene Davenport was killed. For indeed she was murdered. I am no longer the seventeen-year-old girl, eager for a life in the theater who stood in the wings and witnessed it all. Although in my heart and mind, I feel I am still that young woman even though the image I see in the mirror tells me otherwise.

In this modern world of 1951, it would be difficult to find anyone who would even remember Irene's name—especially since the advent of moving pictures and the creation of so many "stars"; so much opportunity for fame that was unheard of in Irene Davenport's day. Of course, it is impossible for me to ever forget her.

Looking back, as famous as she was, certainly the most famous part of Irene's life was her death. That took place center stage, in front of twenty-six hundred people, as well

as those of us in the cast who stood backstage and watched,
paralyzed in disbelief. Sometimes things happen so quickly
that one cannot simply think, nor act fast enough. The brain
is not able to engage the body, I suppose.

But, all that is, as we say, backstory.

When my beloved great-grandniece, Agnes, insisted
that I record the events of my life and my memories of
them, I was resistant. I thought that it was a misplaced idea,
a lot of nonsense. Who would want to hear the history of an
actress who, after all, had spent the bulk of her theatrical
career as a "second banana"?

But, she is a persistent and loveable thorn in my side.
After all, she is the only one in my entire family who has
ever exhibited any kind of talent (or interest) in my
profession. A lovely child, she is beginning her own career
as an actress and I know she will do well. Unfortunately,
she has been burdened with what I believe is a horrid name
and moreover, should have been named after me—either
Rosemary or Lillian would have been much more suitable.
However, her mother is a McKenzie and that bunch has
always been rather high-minded and overly impressed
with themselves. (I am indeed sorry if this offends you, dear
Agnes, but you know this from your own experience to be
true.)

And so, for Agnes, I begin the first installment of my
memoir. Living as I do just north of Chicago in a small
cottage on the Lake Forest estate of my dear brother, my
every need met, I find myself with more than enough time
on my hands to take pen to paper. Agnes wants to know
what life was like when I was her age and how and why I
went into the theater. She wants to know about my

challenges, experiences, triumphs and failures. Her questions have focused my thoughts on those memories—some pleasant and others, not so pleasant, but all a part of who I became—and how I got to where I am now, at the inconceivable age of ninety-seven.

I have always loved Chicago. It is the city of my birth and the home of my family. It is also the birthplace of my career, indeed my life, in the theater, which took place in that awful fall of 1871—but more about that later.

Chicago possesses a wonderful energy. And I connect my love for the city with my Father. He loved Chicago so much and he was an influential part of the expansion of the city.

He and I always had a special relationship. Often, he would remark to me—or anyone else in the family who could bear to listen—that I had a terrible curiosity about things that were none of my business. This was very true. My older brother, John William, said that it made me a horrible snoop. I often got myself into a world of trouble because of this curiosity. Normal people often felt my intense interest in them was impolite, if not downright rude; theater people, of course, felt differently.

The truth is that *people*, especially, their thoughts and actions, fascinate me. The more I watch, observe and study them, the more captivated I become. Human behavior just plain intrigues me. I have to know *why* people do what they do. I must confess that it has also helped me to develop my own sense of humor. If you can look at another's behavior with a sense of the absurd, with a sense of the joy in what *you* do, what *they* do can become quite amusing. Although my mother frequently professed that she did not completely understand my particular humorous appreciation of life, she did feel it was vital for me to have such an outlook. As she often told me, "Rosemary (for Lillian was my stage name and Mother never deigned to use it, always calling me by my full, given name and never a shortened version), you are not and never will be beautiful. You are *attractive*."

As if that, somehow, was the better of the two. Nonetheless, I have to admit that I agreed with Mother's assessment of my looks. I am not particularly beautiful. I prefer to think of myself as a chameleon. However, I really can become quite beautiful once costumed and properly made up when undertaking the persona of a character.

Interestingly enough, there is quite a difference of opinion among actors about this process. In his wonderful biography, Mr. Joseph Jefferson III—in my opinion, one of the greatest actors America has ever produced (save, of course, Edwin Booth, who was and always will remain my absolute favorite, but more of him at a later date)—always made the most sense to me. He often spoke about how he advocated acting with "a cool head and a warm heart." That is the methodology I have tried to employ throughout my career.

Well, as always, I can see that I have already wandered a little far from the point. However, I do have to say, in hindsight, that the attributes observed early on by both Mother and Father have stood by me very well in a life spent in the theater.

But, I digress once again—an attribute of my advanced age, I believe.

Perhaps, like all good stories, I should begin at the very beginning. Although, for me, the beginning of my theatrical life began, *truly* began, with the death of Irene Davenport. I had such a hunger for performing on stage. It was a craving that was likely to be denied. As the only daughter of an upper class Chicago family, I might as well have had a passion to fly to the moon. But Irene's death propelled me into a new life that became a strange and wonderful odyssey on so many levels.

I suppose the fact that I was born in Chicago in the late winter of 1854 is an appropriate place to start, but it hardly seems relevant to my story. For, I have always let it be known to the public that I am a full ten years younger than my birth date would lead one to believe—a wise course of action for any woman involved in so public a career field (and I urge you, dear Agnes, to remember it). I have also worked very hard to maintain that myth, particularly when interviewed by producers. Since there is little chance that anyone else will ever read this memoir, I have no problem confessing the truth at this juncture.

However, I wish to begin with the New York theatrical Christmas season of 1866. Any true memoir should start at the real beginning and, for me, the commencement of my true life started when I was twelve. The journey that brought me to stand onstage of the Grand Theater as Lillian Nolan, novice, *aspiring* actress (performing as the Gentlewoman attending on Lady Macbeth, no less *and* with one line), began with my beloved grandmother, Eleanor Lillian Nolan Hampton. I became her namesake when I took her name on as an actress. A wonderful, *forceful* woman, she was the matriarch of my father's family. Of average height and build for a woman of the time, she had the most beautiful white hair which was always exquisitely coiffed. You would think that would have made her look older than she was but for some reason she always appeared younger than her age. She ruled over her six adult children with grace, wit, and subtle blackmail. With them she was always reserved. With me it was otherwise. I was her blatant favorite and she expressed her love for me freely and easily. She was the family eccentric and I loved her for it. I was very much like her. She adored me and that adoration was completely and utterly returned.

She lived in a very large and elegant home on the North Side of Chicago on Ohio Street. My family's comfortable domicile—a wedding gift to my parents from my grandmother—was located a mere three blocks away. The nearness of which I am sure, Mother appreciated to no end. However, I was eternally grateful for the proximity.

My grandmother had coerced my parents into letting me go with her to New York as a Christmas treat, skillfully outmaneuvering them and providing for me what turned out to be a miraculous experience. What a trip that was! My first long distance train ride, my first stay in a hotel, my first time in New York and my first time in a theater—all rolled into one Christmas package. New York, at that time, was a place so removed from my world in Chicago that it may well have been another country all together. And, in some ways, it was.

My grandmother possessed many friends and had a wide range of interests, but her particular passion was the theatrical world. It was from that special circle of friends that I was to benefit, in immeasurable ways. For that memorable holiday in New York in December of 1866, my grandmother had obtained tickets to see Charlotte

Cushman as Queen Katherine in *Henry VIII* (one of several of Charlotte Cushman's farewell tours). I sat in the box my grandmother had secured and leaned forward in my seat. I do not remember who played Henry VIII. I do not remember the dress I wore, the temperature of the theater, or indeed what the theater looked like. I only remember Charlotte. It was if she had pulled my deepest yearnings for what I wanted and desired from the very fiber of my being and spoke them aloud. Those hours spent with Charlotte changed my life. It was then that my future became set. All my longing coalesced into one focused desire: a life in the theater and on the stage.

Her performance was formidable. She acted the role of the beleaguered queen with incredible understanding, revealing an extraordinary woman of strength and integrity. At least, it seemed that way to me. I knew after that performance that I was meant to do the same. A flame ignited in my being to do as Charlotte Cushman did; to be the woman she was and have all she had. I begged my grandmother to take me back to see her again. She was amused and obligingly agreed. We saw three more performances of *Henry VIII*. That was a fateful experience for me. I began to awaken to my true purpose in life: to be an actress and create the same kind of magic that Charlotte Cushman created in front of an audience.

Because of her connections and patronage, my grandmother was acquainted with Charlotte Cushman and was able to take me backstage to meet her. She was a formidable woman. Tall, with a square face and heavy eyebrows, she was not at all pretty in the popular sense, but she exuded great energy and an imposing life force. In her presence, my passion for what I really wanted to do with my life fully burst forth upon me. When I blurted out that I wanted to be an actress, my grandmother laughed aloud, but Charlotte Cushman looked into my eyes.

"You have a strong and earnest spirit," she said. "You have the true religion of labor in your heart. Therefore, I have no fears for you; let what will come, come."

And then, she pulled me close and whispered into my ear, "You can succeed at whatever you wish, if you have the will to do it."

I went away from that experience a changed girl. My life lay in front of me and I finally knew what I had to do.

My grandmother later told me that Charlotte's father had lost all his money when she was in her teens. She became the financial support for what was a large and extended family. Charlotte was a woman who had achieved much and done it through sheer necessity, determination, and talent. It made me admire her all the more.

On our final night in New York, Grandmother took me to see Edwin Booth in a production of *Hamlet*. Grandmother had been in Ford's theater the night that Mr. Booth's brother, John Wilkes Booth, shot Mr. Lincoln. It was an experience she never forgot. After that national tragedy, many people hated actors and the theater and, of course, it was a great personal heartbreak for the Booth family, as well. Grandmother had a longer view of things, and she so loved theater—every bit of it. Whenever certain theater people were in Chicago, she would invite them to her home. She was famous in her own right for the salons she held.

With all the other actors she knew, she always held a special place in her heart for Edwin Booth. He was in his mid-thirties and at the very pinnacle of his abilities at the time of the murder of Mr. Lincoln. He gave up the stage because of his brother's vile act, but by the winter of 1866, he had returned to the only livelihood he had ever known. Hamlet was his most famous role. Sadness seemed to surround and pervade his performance as I watched him. The only thing I remember about that night was that presence. When he was on stage, I could not take my eyes from him. His performance was magical. In all my many years of performing and watching other performers, no one ever approached what Edwin Booth could do with a role for an audience. He was magnificent.

On the trip back to Chicago, I resolved to become an actress. Have you ever wanted something so badly that you were willing to do anything to obtain it? I don't just mean that it would be nice to have or that you wanted it like you wanted a new hat or a dress or to go someplace nice. No, this was a longing that erupted from my heart. It was a deep ache that originated in my soul. I had no knowledge of how, when, or in what way my longing would be fulfilled. I only knew the theater was calling to me and that it was my calling in life. I had to take heed and pursue it, no matter what obstacles may lay in my path, no matter what sacrifice it demanded of me.

Where I got this yearning, I certainly don't know. It was most assuredly not part of my bloodline. My entire family, save my beloved grandmother, was absolutely appalled by the idea. In point of fact, Grandmother was not exceptionally keen on the idea either.

The theater began to pound in my blood. When I got home, I wrote "actress" out on a piece of paper and below that word, the advice that Charlotte had whispered to me. Over the next few years, I carried that paper around with me in my pocket. Whenever I became discouraged, I would put my hand into my pocket and curl my fingers around that piece of paper. I would hold it tightly and those words would flow through my mind with such conviction that I knew I was not to be denied! Such a hunger, such an overwhelming desire, it became the driving force of my life. I know my dear Agnes has it, too, and she is the only one in my family other than myself to feel it.

I was going to be an actress and on that score, I was adamant. From that time onward, my only desire was to see as many plays and performers as possible. Since Grandmother had box seats at several fine Chicago theaters, and we enjoyed each other's company, this was not too much of a problem.

I began to mimic how I thought Charlotte Cushman would interpret the roles I saw on stage. I began to put on "plays," dragging my tolerant younger brother, Francis, into service to play all supporting roles. However, it was some years into my career before I realized I could not be Charlotte Cushman, for alas, I did not possess her scope of talent. That was to be my personal tragedy and one that took me many years in which to reconcile myself. But, that is a topic for another time.

No one knows where my sense of the dramatic came from or how it emerged. Certainly not from Father, who was the most pragmatic of men. Always impeccably dressed, he cut an imposing figure. We shared the same hazel eyes, face shape, and I was close to his height. I thought that was all we shared. He was as formidable as the building on State and Washington where he worked as Vice-President of the First National Bank. Constructed from stone and steel, the building was said to be fireproof. Customers felt completely confident that their money was safe there. Patrons always felt exactly the same kind of conviction about their security with Father, as well. He emanated that assurance in himself and his world.

Mother was quite beautiful, the most demure and proper of women. I'm sure it was a disappointment to her that her only daughter was not more like her—either in physical expression or temperament. However, I chose to place at least part of the responsibility for my talent at her feet. When reprimanding either myself or my siblings, she always managed to pause, lower her voice and, in a most dramatic tone, finish whatever she had to say. Usually including some sort of dire consequences should we not follow her specific advice. It was a device, I have to say, I learned to use to some effect in my career on the stage. Her rendition always sent chills down my backbone and prompted immediate and complete obedience.

After I was well on the pathway to my career in the theater, Mother once told me, in a moment of keen emotional disturbance (brought on by myself), that I had disgraced my family due to the licentious act of becoming an actress and God only knew what would become of me—using that exact and foreboding tone of voice. But, I believe she actually planted the dramatic seed in me with her own awe-inspiring performances.

It quickly became obvious that my parents were not as amused as Grandmother in my focused desire to become an actress. As I became older, it was made abundantly clear to me that my parents had other plans for me and their hopes were not high. I was not beautiful, in the accepted fashion, but I did have an assured future as the lovely wife of some appropriate man—preferably lawyer or banker—with whom I would have lovely children and who would take me off their hands. While I had no intention of following their plans, my first acting role developed out of the necessity to lead them into believing I agreed with them.

As a child, I had always been rather stubborn. Father said Mother indulged me far too much. Mother insisted it was quite the other way around.

"An actress? Impossible!" Mother would say.

With a surreptitious look at me, Father whispered to Mother, "You know the type of woman who chooses that life!"

This piqued my interest even more.

"What type?" I asked.

Mother hushed me and shooed me from the parlor, closing the pocket doors that rolled shut in perfect balance, emerging from the walls where they were safely secured and rarely closed. Their voices were heard only in murmur, and no matter how closely I pressed my ear to the solid oak of those doors, I could not hear what they were saying.

This frightened me more than anything else did, because it appeared that my parents were in complete agreement. In my experience, Father had always been my champion and Mother always gave in to him. Their agreement was so unusual an experience that I knew it was to have profound consequences for my life. Indeed, it took me five years to understand the full scope of their plans.

In comparison with me, my other siblings were perfectly normal. Both my brothers chose very acceptable paths in life and easily met the overwhelming approval of both of our parents. Of course, I was of great benefit to my brothers because Mother or Father could point at me and say, "Thank the Lord, you are not like your sister."

Just after my birthday, I read in the paper that Augustin Daly was putting together a production of *Macbeth,* which would star Irene Davenport and Edward Hearne. It was a touring package company and they would pick up the rest of the cast when they came to Chicago in the fall for rehearsal and production. This was it. I *had* to be in that cast. I did the only sensible thing I could think of doing—I went to see Grandmother.

I'll never forget how unseasonably warm the weather was. The daffodils were up early that spring and yellow had always been my favorite color. As I walked the three blocks over to Grandmother's home, the total optimism of youth took over me and I felt that the smell of the flowers and the sound of the birdsong of spring were portends that all that was cold and dark was truly behind me and the future was bright. When I appeared at her door, I was immediately granted entrance. It was early afternoon and I had interrupted one of her salons. She always had time for me.

"Come in and join us!" she said.

There was a group of ladies of her general age in attendance in her parlor—wealthy matrons like herself—all with whom I was well-acquainted.

"You all know my granddaughter, Rosemary," she said.

In the middle of the group was a much younger woman at least twenty years junior to the youngest of the women in attendance. Her manner was also very youthful and she was extremely beautiful.

"Now Rosemary, you know everyone here except Cora. Cora, dear, this is my granddaughter, Rosemary Hampton."

"How do you do Miss Hampton?" Cora said.

Her manner was exceptionally polite and I was a little taken aback.

"Rosemary, this is Cora L. V. Tappan."

Grandmother said her name, as if she were someone I should know, someone exceptional. I wracked my brain for some actress by that name, but knew she couldn't possibly be famous. I knew the name of every famous thespian at the time and even the lesser ones and her name was not among them. Who was she? I could tell my grandmother was greatly amused by my ignorance. But, it was Cora herself who answered my unspoken question.

"Ah, you are wondering perhaps if I am an actress. No, not at all. I am a Spiritualist," she said.

It unnerved me that my thoughts were so transparent, and it flitted across my mind that I should guard my expression in the future. I had no idea what a Spiritualist was. Our family was strictly Presbyterian, with the exception of Grandmother who had become Unitarian and attended Unity Church. I had never heard this term before. I had no idea what it meant. The training pounded into me by my mother was my only saving grace.

"How very nice," I said, politely.

This seemed to amuse the entire group and I was the source of much laughter. Grandmother asked me to wait in the second parlor as they were just finishing their "meeting."

I went into the second parlor. It was ordinarily my favorite room, but I was so agitated, so seventeen years old and in the throes of knowing how right I was, so passionate about what I wanted, I could not appreciate the room. I threw myself on the deep green velvet sofa and stared up at the ceiling. Time dragged by—it must have been only five minutes but seemed more like five hours to me—when I sensed someone standing in the doorway. Grandmother, at last! But, it was the Spiritualist, Cora.

"Your grandmother asked me to come and wait with you as she says her farewells to the rest of her guests," she said.

Even then, I could hear the ritual leave-taking the women were making in the foyer as they said their goodbyes to one another. Cora came into the room.

"Do you know what Spiritualism is?" she asked.

I had to admit I didn't.

"Well, I have the ability to contact the Beyond."

Beyond what? I wondered.

She laughed. I hadn't realized that I had said that out loud! Her laughter had a wonderful quality to it and I relaxed. You couldn't help but like someone who had such a wonderful laugh. It was warm, light, and joyful.

"By 'the Beyond,' I mean the other side of the veil...those who have passed. I can contact them and the people I meet with can ask questions and I get the answers."

"Really?" I asked. "Like my grandfather? He died when I was little."

"Just so," she said. "Matter of fact, that is what brought your grandmother to me—the hope that I could make contact with him."

I wanted to ask if she had succeeded when Grandmother appeared in the doorway to the parlor.

"Oh, you are making friends. Lovely. We all know Rosemary wants to be an actress, but can you tell us anything we may not know, Cora?"

That wonderful laugh again.

"Eleanor, you know her better than I, but she has a passionate fire within her and she will follow it. Best to let her have her way."

I was stunned. I never expected this—a stranger to be my ally!

She turned to me and said, "I really must go now, but, dear Rosemary, I know we shall meet again. I will be back in Chicago in the autumn and I expect we shall see each other then. Goodbye, it was so nice meeting you."

We all walked out to the foyer and my grandmother said her goodbyes—then, she turned to me.

"Well, I expect you came for some support. I wasn't about to give it, but now, I am thinking differently."

"Oh, Grandmother," I wailed, "If you don't help me, who will?"

It was that very afternoon that she agreed to write to her friend, Mr. Augustin Daly, to see what could be done—if anything. At the time, Mr. Daly was one of the foremost theatrical managers in the country. His taste and attention to detail were legendary. A perfectionist, his productions always achieved high artistic merit. From the depths of despair, my spirits soared to unimaginable heights. I was as good as on the professional stage! I threw my arms around her and hugged her with all the enthusiasm I felt.

"No promises, mind you. I cannot control what Mr. Daly does, but he might be willing to do a favor for an old friend and supporter. Of course, convincing your parents is another matter entirely."

I knew then that I was on my way.

As things turned out, a series of events occurred that propelled me into taking immediate and I have to say, *dramatic* action. I found myself engaged to be married. Only, it wasn't of my choosing. My parents concocted this scheme because they thought it would be good for me. Only two months after my seventeenth birthday, I became cognizant of the full extent of my parents' plans for me.

My father had an important client, a man with a considerable amount of money invested in the First National Bank by the name of Mr. James Walden. He was married to a woman who was quite often ill and it seemed to me that she secretly reveled in the attention it brought her. They had one son over whom they doted. Their family had been invited, fed and entertained in our home many times over the years. The son, James Jr., was four years older than I and was now out of college and set to join in his father's business concerns. James Sr. was inordinately proud of his heir and planned that together they would rule his entire business empire—which was substantial. It was both sets of parents' heartfelt desire that James Jr. and I should wed. That this idea was abhorrent to me had no impact whatsoever on their plans.

This led to many shed tears (mostly mine) and arguments with Mother and Father, in which I am afraid I told them I hated them and would never forgive them should they make me marry James Jr. Their tactic was to assure me that because they loved me, they knew what was best for me. However, should I decline to wed James Jr., *they* most assuredly would never forgive *me*.

Oh, the tears! Oh, the arguments! Oh, the confinement to my bedroom! Talk about drama. There was no necessity for performance—I lived it. My parents had a great deal of faith in their ability to persuade me into their course of action, mainly having to do with spending long days and nights alone in my room. I did not garner my release until I finally agreed to at least meet James Jr.

So, one late June day, he was invited to dinner. From my many years of acquaintance with James Jr., I always found him to be irritating, obnoxious, and rather pompous. And now, I was aghast to discover that he apparently had set his mind on marriage to me! I was a suitable girl who would indeed be most fortunate to marry into his family and it was through this great largess that I was to be eternally grateful to him.

This was a boy with whom I had played as a child, whose left eye I had accidentally blackened when I was eight and he was twelve. Although, I have to say his manners had improved greatly. When he appeared at the door, he brought flowers for Mother! He was positively ingratiating to Father.

I girded my loins for battle and prepared myself to fire, should I be fired upon. My older and younger siblings were there, as well, and it was a solace to me that we enjoyed a shared opinion of James Jr. Throughout the seemingly endless dinner for which James Jr. had been specifically invited, my siblings and I surreptitiously exchanged significant glances when some particularly pompous remark was made. John William, my older brother, was just nineteen and preparing for his first year at Northwestern University and my younger brother, Francis, was thirteen. It was truly wonderful having brothers. It gave me a whole other perspective on the male mind, which I certainly would not have had access to had my parents given me sisters.

It wasn't until after dinner was over that the first rally was fired.

"Rosemary," Mother said so sweetly, "take James Jr. into the front parlor and show him the lovely new photographs your father had taken of our trip to Mackinac Island."

I looked up at Mother in surprise.

What is she talking about, I wondered. *Me, entertain James Jr.?*

Honestly, looking back now, I see I was nowhere near the astute woman of the world I thought myself to be. Since I knew my career on the stage was just a letter away, I was amenable to anything and that included a few moments alone with James Jr. before dessert was served.

The front parlor was our formal entertaining room. Mother had exquisite taste and this room showcased her talent for home decor. The furniture was lovely, in the height of fashion, but amazingly comfortable. I always felt at ease in that room. White lace curtains hung in the windows that overlooked our lawn and the row of mature elms that grew right up to Ohio Street. There was a feeling of peace and contentment that normally would overtake me in this room. Of all the rooms in the house, including my own bedroom, this parlor was the room in which I felt most at home. Except for this moment with James Jr. He sat on the sofa—my favorite place—and I sat on the upright chair my mother usually used. I reached for the album Father had put together and resided on a side table.

"Never mind about that," James Jr. said. "You silly goose, it's one of the things I like best about you—not a brain in your head!"

Taken aback by this extraordinary compliment, I was about to protest when he stopped me in my tracks.

"You know why we're here alone, don't you?"

I was beginning to feel suspicious, but once again, James Jr. did my talking for me and apparently, my thinking as well.

"Our parents want us to get married," he said.

Of course, I knew this, but preferred to live in denial, instead relying on the expectation of a reply from Mr. Daly, which I was sure would come at any time.

With that, he rose, came to my chair, knelt, pulled a small dark velvet box from his jacket and opened it. It held a gold ring with a sizeable bluish-green stone at the center surrounded by two small pearls.

"I know diamonds are becoming much more fashionable, but my mother—who has a perfect sense of what's exactly right, which you will come to appreciate more as you get to know her more intimately as a second mother to you—suggested this tourmaline. She remembered your hazel eyes, you know."

At that particular moment, I didn't know a thing about my hazel eyes, but I knew my jaw had dropped and my mouth was wide open in a particularly unappealing way.

"Whaaaa–" I moaned.

"Oh, silly girl, I've always thought you were acceptable and a man like me, in my position, needs a wife from a good family. You know you're not unattractive and since I've always thought you amusing, and my mother said we would make a good match, here."

And, with that, he grabbed my left hand and attempted to shove what I can only describe as the ugliest piece of jewelry I had ever seen on the third finger of my left hand. With some effort, I reclaimed my hand from his grasp.

"James Jr., you do me such an honor by your heartfelt proposal, but I am truly afraid I must decline."

It was James Jr.'s turn to become a slack-jawed yokel.

"But, it's all arranged."

"Not by me," I said. I stood up.

He jumped to his feet. "Of course you'll marry me."

"James Jr., what would possess me to do that? You don't even like me."

He paused. That got his attention and he frowned.

"That's not true. I've always felt you…liked me—and my parents have wanted this for so long."

It was beyond my ken how he had created this piece of fiction in his mind—for it could exist nowhere else—that I could possibly be attracted to him. However, I could only say, "Well, no one told me."

He looked so abashed that I had to take pity on him.

"Look, James, we're so different. We want such different things. We really wouldn't suit together, you know. Not really."

"Oh, so you think I'm not good enough for you! I will be very rich one day and my future wife will benefit from that. You won't find better than me and my prospects."

"James, I didn't mean that."

"I believe you did."

Did I? I didn't think I did. I thought I just didn't want to get married at all, so I told him that.

"Actually, James, I just don't want to marry at all. My plan is to become an actress."

"That! You don't have a chance of becoming an actress—it would ruin your reputation and break your parents' hearts. Besides, you're just not pretty enough to be an actress."

I had imparted my deepest desire to him and not only did he throw it back in my face, but he insulted me in the bargain! That did it.

"James, if you were the last man on earth, I wouldn't marry you. You are an insensitive, pompous boor and I wouldn't have you on a silver platter."

That was the only part of the discussion my parents heard, as they chose, at that very moment, to step into the room. James Jr.'s face turned the deepest shade of scarlet. For a moment, I became concerned for his health, as I thought there was an exceptionally good chance he might just explode. Instead, he snapped shut the lid on the velvet box, turned and stomped out of the room. Mother went after him and I could hear her trying to soothe him, but he completely ignored her.

The next thing I heard was the slam of the front door and Mother burst into tears. And they could not understand my propensity for the theater, surrounded by all this drama; I truly felt I was a natural! I turned to Father who was still standing there. As I said, I had always had a special relationship with my father and expected him to understand my feelings now. As Grandmother's son, I felt he was more like her. I knew I was his favorite child, as I was the only girl, the one to whom he was most indulgent. I knew he would be my ally.

"Father," I began.

"No," he said.

Just that one word.

Mother's voice was one of fury though her tears.

"We have allowed this theatrical fantasy long enough. You have embarrassed us all tonight, young lady. Refusing a perfectly acceptable, perfectly respectable offer of marriage—and in such a way! Shame!"

Once again, I looked to Father. I could see no support there. He looked me straight in the face and I am ashamed to say I could not hold his gaze. As I looked down, he said, "You will apologize to James Jr. and to us and you will marry him or you will never see the outside of your room until you are thirty."

I was completely taken aback. I had never seen Father like this. Of course, I had never crossed purposes with him. Was it so with all men? My mind began to chew on this problem—could I be in such error? I tried once more.

"Father, I really can't marry James Jr."

"You can and you will."

It was then that I noticed how truly angry he was. He was giving me no quarter, no room for compromise. I fled the parlor, ran past my weeping Mother, up the stairs and into the haven of my own room where I threw myself on the bed. There I let loose my own emotions, proving that I was indeed my Mother's daughter.

But screw your courage to the sticking-place,
And we'll not fail

Macbeth Act I, Scene 7

~~~~~~

CHAPTER TWO

The next few weeks were, for the most part, more boring than anything else. The only light moment came when John William stuck a note under my door, which wholeheartedly supported my position in turning down James Jr. It also included a very fine caricature of my proposed fiancé that showcased his large and not particularly aristocratic nose. It was my only solace. No one came to see me and no one talked to me. Trays of food were brought to my room by Jane, our housemaid, and then, taken away. I was held completely apart from Grandmother and received no communication from her. Did she support me? Or did she hate me now, as I felt my parents so obviously did. Oh, why didn't they understand? I was so alone.

I knew I had to come up with a plan of my own, one that would appease my parents, but, at the same time, allow me the freedom to leave my locked room. I decided the weakest link—the most emotional one—was Mother. I knew, however, she was not a stupid woman, and so, I had to appeal to her on just the right level, to utilize just the right strategy for her to believe me. I decided to tell her I would accept James Jr., but I wanted something in return: a last fling, if you will, with Grandmother. I had to know where Grandmother stood and if all was truly lost. I wanted Mother to believe that all I wanted was to have a last chance to immerse myself in the world of theater and then, I would accept the wishes of my parents.

When Jane appeared the next morning with my breakfast tray I put on a visage of utmost remorse. I asked her humbly if she thought Mother would have time to speak with me. Very shortly thereafter, there was a light tapping—as if I could allow entrance—on the door that was locked from the outside and then that same lock was turned. Mother walked in and I immediately had the sense that she was trying to put on a good show as the stern and caring mother, as well as dutiful wife, but she was really at the breaking point herself. Interesting, what a theatrical perspective on life can do for you to understand human behavior.

"Jane said you wanted to see me."

At that moment, I knew. I knew with all my heart and soul that this was the greatest acting opportunity of my life to date. If I could convince her of my change of mind, of my acceptance and acquiescence to the marriage to James Jr., then I truly was destined for a life on the stage. If I couldn't do that, then all I was good for, all I deserved was marriage to such a one as James Jr.

I took a deep breath and arranged my body and face in terms of abject sorrow and repentance. I practically threw myself on the floor at her knees.

"Please, Mother! I am so sorry, so very sorry for the hurt and pain that I have caused you and Father."

While this was true to some extent, these actual words were spoken by the heroine of a melodrama that Grandmother and I had seen about three months ago. It was uncanny, but it worked. Mother immediately softened, lifted me up and put her arms around me.

"Oh, Rosemary, we only want what is best for you."

Yes, I knew that, but I also knew they had *no* idea of what was best for me—only I did. Instead, I humbly replied, "I know that now, Mother."

"And you will accept James Jr., won't you?"

"Yes, Mother."

A shudder went through me, involuntarily, but Mother took it as the extreme emotion and sensitivity I was feeling at this moment.

"All I ask is one more theater trip with Grandmother."

Mother pulled back.

I rushed in with my explanation.

"I know James Jr. doesn't like the theater and I'm sure I won't get to go. Allow me this last trip and I'll do what you ask."

"Oh, Rosemary, I don't know if I can get your Father to agree to that."

"Please, Mother, one more trip and I'll do anything you ask."

She looked me in the eye and I am somewhat proud to admit, even from the vantage point of so many years later, that I never flinched.

Since that time, I have come to understand a good part of acting is in the eyes. If you can believe what and whom you are, and someone looks you in the eye and believes it to be true as well, you have got them convinced. And so it was with Mother.

Sweet freedom! The only price to pay was reconciliation with James, Jr. This led to yet another dinner. This time, the atmosphere at the dining table was excruciatingly painful and reserved. And I also knew my acting skills were really starting to be honed as I appeared quite contrite under the watchful eyes of both Mother and Father and condescended to everything James Jr. said.

When we were once again alone in the parlor, I apologized and very nicely, if not beautifully, requested his forgiveness (once more recalling the words of the heroine from the above mentioned melodrama). My heart fluttered with hope for a brief moment when I thought he would accept the apology, but forego the proposal. That hope was completely dashed. I politely, albeit without enthusiasm, allowed him to place that ugly ring on the third finger of my left hand. We were officially engaged.

Of course, this sent him into elevated heights of pompousness, but the price was worth it.

This event completely confused my dear brothers and John William was very disappointed, believing that I had lost my mind to accept James Jr., but I had to make the best of it. It was just not possible for me to offer him any explanation without jeopardizing my plans.

When I finally did get to meet Grandmother again, things did not go as I would have liked, because Father insisted on being present. We met at Grandmother's house and my first clue that she was on my side was that she had her cook prepare Father's favorite macaroon cookies. He only got these on special occasions, such as his birthday and Christmas.

When he protested that she was trying to "butter him up," she merely said, "My dear Walter, this *is* a special occasion. We are about to celebrate the engagement of your only daughter."

That did seem to appease him and he relaxed and helped himself to several of the cookies. I was on pins and needles because I desperately needed to talk to Grandmother, but had to be patient. I was in agony acting the role of the complacent newly-engaged young woman.

It was wonderful to be so loved, to know that I had a person in my life that I could be myself with and be accepted unconditionally, but it was rather stressful with Father being there. Of course, I knew he loved me, as well. It was just that certain conditions came with it. So we talked, the three of us, of what I would term rather boring and mundane things like the selection of a wedding dress, the current fashions of lace, fabric and other accessories. I attempted to convey as much enthusiasm as humanly possible.

Grandmother was not fooled. She knew me too well. But, it was far too much for Father. Convinced we would be immersed in the discussion of these delightful and appropriate frivolities, he believed that the two of us were genuinely happy and excited about the forthcoming nuptials.

It was with great inner relief to me when he finally turned to us and smiled.

"Dear Mama, as entertaining and pleasant as it is to be in your company, I have been away from the office for too long. Please see that Rosemary gets home by three," he said.

Grandmother immediately agreed to this plan, promising faithfully that I would arrive at home not a moment past three. Then, she wrapped up the remaining cookies in one of her fine linen napkins for him to take with and enjoy at his office. They walked into the foyer and he gave her an embrace, a perfunctory kiss on the check and was gone.

I watched from the parlor window as he began the walk down Ohio Street. When Grandmother came back into the room, she sighed and said, "I love that boy, but I thought he would never leave. Now, what's all this about you marrying James Jr.?"

"Oh, Grandmother!"

I threw myself at her and burst into true tears of misery. Patting my back, she led me to the couch, sat me down and handed me another one of her napkins.

"Now, now, is it really all that bad?"

It was the end of the world! The end of *my* world—as I saw it and, here I was looking to her for a way out. She hadn't said a word about helping me or whether or not she had heard from Mr. Daly. I wiped my streaming eyes with her immaculate white napkin and gazed imploringly up at her.

"Oh Grandmother, he is awful. So full of himself and Mother and Father are insistent that I marry him. I would rather throw myself into Lake Michigan and drown."

Grandmother paused.

"That is rather a bit too much. Try to get hold of yourself, dear Rosemary. I just wanted to be sure. Now, stop your crying because I have received a bit of news that just may be of interest to you."

It is amazing how life can turn on one event or one piece of information. How you can wake up in despair and then, get one tiny piece of information and your day—or even your life—completely and utterly changes for the better. For me, it was the telegram Grandmother pulled from her pocket. She had received a reply from her query to Mr. Daly.

It has been more than eighty years since I stood in the front parlor and stared at the paper in her hand, but I can remember it vividly now. Time seemed to stop as Grandmother read that telegram to me:

> *Delighted to receive your letter STOP In the process of creating a tour with the magnificent Irene Davenport and Edward Hearne STOP Would be pleased to offer your granddaughter $3 a week as a supernumerary for the duration of the time in Chicago STOP*
>
> *—Augustin Daly*

Have there ever been any other sweeter words? The realization of my hopes and dreams—to become reality! Grandmother watched as I literally jumped up and down and danced around her parlor.

Then, she asked me a question that startled me right out of my euphoria.

"Are you sure this is what you really want, Rosemary?"

I asked what she meant. She held out the telegram.

"You are at a turning point in your life, my dear. You need to recognize it and finally understand the significance of this event. On the one hand…" she held out the telegram to me. "You have one opportunity, which leads who knows where? After this, you will need to find another position and then another…the actor's life is a difficult one."

I told her I was convinced that once started, I would not have a problem getting another position. She frowned at that, but made no disagreement.

"The repercussion of your decision means that your mother and father will disown you. Your brothers will not be allowed to see you. Think about it, Rosemary. Please, please think about it. Actresses have the worst reputation—they are not even welcome in church! Once you go down this path, you cannot go back. You will be a pariah.

"You will be giving it all up—your family's love and support, the assurance of your home, a secure future. You must know that marriage is the only acceptable future. And it is expected for a woman your age. Even to this particular man, if not desirable to you—he is respectable and at the very least, predictable. He is from a good family with a secure future, but you are giving that up and for what? Do you really know?"

Logic dictated that she was right. However, I was so young and so convinced of my own abilities, so certain of a glowing future that, with little thought and all emotion, I chose life in the theater. It was what I truly wanted and, although it has not been the easiest path, all things considered, had I to go back to that moment of choice, I would make the same decision all over again. In that, my fate was, and has always been, sealed.

Once again, I was grateful for Grandmother's love. I knew she did not agree with my choice. She would much rather see me securely, lovingly married and producing great-grandchildren. But, she loved me enough to let me have what I wanted for myself. Truly an unusual woman for her age and time, but I couldn't be where I am and who I am today had she not loved me so much.

My decision was met with pain and fury on the part of my parents. At the brink of reconciliation with my "fiancé," I had to tell them that I rejected him once again for my own purposes.

That night, the most awful argument took place between my parents and me; worse than anything that had happened to me in my entire seventeen years of life. I have had many other incidents when I have been the bearer of bad news or something ugly has happened, but that still ranks as the worst. And I brought it on myself.

The blissfully ignorant joy of completely having your own way is something only the young can know. I told my parents that I was not going to marry James Jr., and that I had accepted a role in a production of *Macbeth* opening in Chicago in September and starring Irene Davenport. Somewhere in my mind, I think I must have expected them to be happy for me. They looked at me as if I had grown another head.

Father was the first to speak.

"I beg your pardon?" he asked.

I repeated my news.

"And, how did this come about?"

Before I could answer, Grandmother appeared in the doorway and said, "I wrote to Mr. Daly on her behalf."

"You...what?"

"Now, Walter, the girl has her heart set on this."

"I don't care about her heart. I care about the honor and duty of this family. Promises have been made, plans have been devised and, by God, they will be kept!"

Thus, the argument began with the first act encompassing a shouting match of incredible proportions between Father and Grandmother. Each one pushed and pulled to have his or her own way, each one raising his or her voice higher and higher to be heard over the other.

Then, I heard Mother's voice speak and, surprisingly, it was very calm. It shocked Father and Grandmother so much that it brought them to a complete silence.

"An actress's life is a very hard choice, Rosemary. You have no real idea. It is not all admiration; it is work and you, well, you don't know what that is. You will never know what you are going to do next and the women who choose that path are not looked on very well by society."

"I know all of that mother," I said, exasperated.

"No, you don't, Rosemary, you only think you do. You might not care now, but you will care a great deal later on."

"I still want to do it," I stubbornly insisted.

"Very well. Then, you must accept the first consequence of your choice. You are no longer welcome in this house."

And with that, she gracefully rose from the chair near the fireplace where she almost always sat and walked from the room.

I turned to Father, but before I could speak, he, too, stood and said, "On this matter, your mother and I are in complete agreement. You have made your decision; you must abide by ours."

He followed my mother's disappearing form, leaving me and Grandmother alone. I ran up the stairs to my room and found Jane there already packing my clothes. Her face was quite pale and it reflected the feeling that was beginning to form in the pit of my stomach. However, I ignored it and threw some necessities in the small travelling bag Jane had placed on my bed. I told her to send the rest of my things to Grandmother, grabbed the bag, ran down the stairs and met Grandmother in the foyer. She took my elbow and we walked out the front door and I didn't even look back. That's a seventeen-year-old for you!

After my parents informed the Waldens that the engagement was truly off, oddly enough—I heard from Jane, when she brought the last of my clothes over to Grandmother's house—that it was James Jr. who had attempted to placate them. Jane had been in the dining room when she overhead their conversation.

"She'll get over it," James Jr. had said. "Let her be in this play. She'll see it for what it is, but when it's over, she'll come to her senses, see what she has lost and I will be there."

Jane said nothing more, but I knew my parents well enough to be sure that they had practically salivated in gratitude for his generosity. It only hardened my resolve.

Thank God for Grandmother. She was my source of refuge; although she made it clear to me that she was not completely convinced I was doing the right thing. I realize now how hard the family split must have been on her, but then, I was rather arrogant and convinced of my own righteousness.

My parents were as good as their word. I did not see or hear from Mother, Father, John William, or Francis for some time. I was about to live my own personal tragedy and there were no supporting actors. I was to find myself completely alone for the first time in my life.

The love that follows us sometime is our trouble,
Which still we thank as love.

Macbeth Act I, Scene 6

~~~~~~

CHAPTER THREE

Father's word was law in our family. No one ever questioned his decisions, including Mother. Now, as I look back at those events, I realize how difficult it must have been for them. They were left to clean up the mess that I had created. They had to deal with the Waldens, the church, the newspapers, society at large, their friends and our family. While they could put off friends and acquaintances with an explanation that I had had a mere change of heart:

You know how young people are these days.

No, we can't understand it ourselves.

Things are not the same as when we were young, etc., etc., ad nauseum.

The family was another issue entirely. Father had five brothers and sisters who were united in their horror of what I had done. Mother only had one much older brother and I am told he was completely speechless when he heard the news and remained so for quite some time.

Of all of this, I remained quite ignorant. Caught in the tumult of excitement only a seventeen-year-old can feel when she believes she has obtained her heart's desire, I was blissfully unaware of anyone else's pain. Grandmother welcomed me, if not with open arms, for family was of paramount importance to her, with great kindness, understanding and patience, all of which she knew her son did not feel, or possess at the time. She held many reservations about the path on which I was about to embark, but I chose not to listen nor concentrate upon them.

Two days later, a letter arrived at Grandmother's from Father. It was posted. He hadn't even let Jane make the short journey over to Grandmother's so that I could garner extra information from her. It read:

> *Rosemary,*
> *I will not call you dear, as you have made a decision that infuriates and embarrasses your mother and myself, as well as the rest of the family. We have forbidden both of your brothers to mention your name and you must not expect to see them for some considerable time—if ever again. However, we have acquiesced to the belief of James Jr. that, as we all hope, your appearance in this one play will convince you of the error of your ways and you will return home and assume your proper role. However, should you remain on the course you have so recklessly chosen, do not expect forgiveness or acceptance from this quarter. We*

ask that you spare us further embarrassment and
dishonor by refraining from the use of your given
name in the despicable profession you have chosen.
Until such time as you come to your senses, we
wash our hands of you.

It was not signed Father, or even Walter Hampton. But, *Mr. Walter Hampton.*

It was about as cold and as formal as one could imagine. I had to take a deep breath and sit down. I felt as if my heart had been cleaved in two. Unbidden, tears began to stream down my face. I would like to say that, in the excitement of what I was about to do, it did not matter, but the truth was that I loved my family very dearly and, in one blow, I had severed them from me. I had always assumed that Father would get used to the idea of having a daughter who was an actress and when I became famous, he might even be proud of me. For the first time, I was no longer sure of that.

I handed the note to Grandmother and her face saddened as she read it.

"I would not have wished this for you. Your father has forgotten what it is like to want to follow what one feels so strongly driven to do."

I took that as agreement with my decision because I felt so strongly my path was set and I had to follow it, wherever it led me. No letter, no matter how painful could change that.

I wiped the wetness from my face. I was seventeen and it is possible to bounce back from almost anything when you are seventeen, especially if you have your heart's desire directly in front of you. I put that note away and tried my best to forget about it.

I threw myself into preparation for my career. Grandmother had a copy of *Macbeth* in a collection of Shakespeare plays and so I spent my days reading and rereading the play—memorizing every line of it. I was beyond excited when the time came for me to appear at the Grand Theater toward the middle of September.

Grandmother owned a box at this theater and we had enjoyed many wonderful performances here. Built in 1857, the building itself was the epitome of elegance with a spacious portico and graceful columns, which supported an entablature and pediment. The lobby was beautifully painted, with frescoes of Roman gods and goddesses. Inside the theater, every seat was good and the acoustics were wonderful.

The décor was done in blue and gold and I felt like royalty sitting in one of the boxes. The auditorium portion of the theater formed the traditional horseshoe shape and extended from one side of the stage to the other. There were tiers of boxes and galleries arranged on different levels and priced accordingly. The stage itself was over one hundred feet, both in depth and width and the fly space above the stage was almost six stories. There was gas lighting on the stage and in the auditorium. The gas jets were housed in elegant glass lamps that could be brightened or dimmed by regulating the flow. It truly was a wonder. Even more of a wonder was that I was going to stand on that stage; I was going to perform at that theater!

That dry and hot September morning, my stomach churned with excitement as I sat in Grandmother's coach and it was all I could do to stay seated properly. The images of that trip remain a blur as I traveled from the North side, over the river on the Clark Street Bridge to the South side and the theatrical district.

The coachman took me around to the front of the theater on Madison Street and dropped me off at the actor's entrance, which was immediately to the left of the main entrance. I stood for a moment and looked down the alley to the doorway marked "Stage Entrance." I wanted to remember absolutely every sensation about this first experience. Years and many, many stage doors later, the sensation was different. The excitement of starting something new—a new experience, the hope of creating new "magic" was always there—but there is only one first time you do anything. You should tune into that experience, hold and treasure it in your heart, for the level of expectation is never the same again.

Just as I was about to take a step forward a huge, grey tabby cat ran past me, down the alley and up the few steps to the stage door. At that spot, he stopped, turned and looked at me, spoke one "meow," as if to ask "What are you waiting for, you silly girl?" and disappeared through the door, which was slightly ajar.

It broke through my reverie and I had to laugh at how seriously I was taking myself. I followed the cat's path through the alley and, at the door, peeked in. The first thing I saw, after walking through the door, was the cat, sitting on a stool. He appeared as if he were waiting for me.

I went over to him and began to rub his head behind his ears and he arched his back in pleasure.

A voice suddenly said, "Gus doesn't take to everyone. If he likes you, you must be all right."

I turned to see a short, mature, wiry man of indeterminate middle age. His reddish-brown hair was short and curly and there was a smattering of freckles across the bridge of his nose. He was dressed simply in dark pants, a vest and white shirt, the sleeves of which were rolled up.

"Is he your cat?" I asked.

"Oh, no. He's the theater cat, doesn't belong to nobody. Cats see between the worlds—this one and the one beyond. It's his job to protect the place."

I remembered what Cora had said about "the Beyond," but before I could ask him if that was what he meant, he spoke again.

"Cats are very lucky in a theater, you know—unless they run across the stage during a performance. Of course, Gus here would never do that."

As if appalled by the very thought, Gus flicked his tail, jumped down and disappeared into the backstage area.

"I'm Teddy Ryan, the Stage Manager. I run the place during the performances. You must be the new girl." He glanced down at a piece of paper in his hand. "Lillian Nolan. It's one of my jobs to keep track of you. Sign here."

He gestured to a book on a small table where there were spaces for members of the performers, musicians and technicians to sign in and out.

"You're early. Wait for the others on stage and—"

He took a look at the flower corsage I was wearing and burst out, "Good grief girl, what on God's green earth were you thinking by wearing that yellow flower?"

Grandmother always kept fresh flowers in a large vase in the foyer of her home and that morning, I had taken one of the yellow roses from an arrangement and turned it into a corsage.

"Flowers are bad luck in a theater—unless you get them after the end of a performance—but never yellow!"

He reached over, grabbed my corsage off the lapel of my walking suit and threw it in the trash bin.

"Bad enough we have to do this Scottish Play—"

"Do you mean Mac—"

"Never, never say the name of that play unless you are required to do so in a performance," he snapped. "I'm thinking you've already jinxed the whole thing already. Bad luck. Bad luck!"

Abruptly, he turned and walked away.

I stood there, slightly stunned. My introduction to the theater had not gone exactly as I had imagined it would. It was then that I heard a soft, utterly feminine voice from somewhere behind me.

"Don't mind Teddy. He is consumed with theatrical superstition. He's quite an expert on it, really."

I turned to see what I still consider the physical embodiment of an angel. A cloud of blonde hair, a small, but neat figure that was immaculately dressed. With her deep, green eyes and a smile that was both warm and welcoming, there was an almost fairy-like quality about her. She was young, but older than I—perhaps by two or three years—but she seemed far more confident and sure of herself.

"I'm Mary Cosgrove," she said, holding her hand out to me.

I took her hand in mine and shook it. It was small and delicate, like the rest of her, but held unexpected strength.

"Rosemary—uh, Lillian Nolan."

Grandmother insisted that I honor Father's wishes on this point and take a stage name. It wasn't that my own was so mundane, which, of course, it was, but she felt very strongly that I should avoid any damage to the family sensitivities. By that, I knew she meant not embarrass them any *further*. Grandmother argued that if I didn't want to rub salt in the wound of Father's pride, I really needed to have another name. We pondered this for some time until we decided on her mother's name, Lillian, and Grandmother's maiden name, Nolan. Lillian Nolan. I liked it. I could see it on handbills and marquees. It had a certain theatricality to it.

I used it now to introduce myself to Mary Cosgrove, but it didn't come off my tongue as easily as I thought that it would. Mary seemed to disregard my hesitation over my own name and smiled at me. I could not help but be drawn into the warmth of that smile.

"Mary is correct. Teddy is profoundly superstitious, particularly when it comes to the theater, but it has proved strangely helpful at times, so I would not disregard his advice."

Now, that voice I knew—deep, resonant and powerful. I turned and saw Edward Hearne standing directly to my right. He was what could only be described as a beautiful man. His attributes were many and apparent: wavy, dark hair, above average height, slim, impeccably dressed. His face was finely boned with deep-set expressive eyes and a perfectly formed and aristocratic nose under which was an impressive mustache. He carried an ebony cane with a silver lion's head at the top, which gave him an elegant air. I swallowed.

"Edward Hearne, at your service, Miss Nolan."

I had to keep myself from curtseying.

"Very pleased to meet you, Mr. Hearne," I managed to say.

"Charming the girls, are you, Edward? How unusual for you."

We all turned to see Irene Davenport poised in the doorway.

Edward sighed under his breath and I thought I heard him murmur, "The queen must have her entrance."

His smile was warm, even if it didn't reach his eyes and he immediately moved toward her and reached out to take her hand and lead her backstage.

"As lovely as always Irene. You brighten all our days with your presence. Such an honor to serve with you."

Even I thought that was a bit much, but Mrs. Davenport seemed to soak it up.

"Let others say what they may, you are never without presence, Edward."

She dropped his hand and swept past the rest of us, completely ignoring Mary and me, and called out to no one in particular.

"Where is Andrew? Ah, there you are. Can we begin?"

Andrew Portman, Mr. Daly's personal representative, hurried toward her from the other side of the stage. A short man with a chubby face and portly frame, he had jet black hair and dark brown eyes. He was dressed in a summer weight nondescript grey suit.

It seemed to me that he was about to bow in front of her before he caught himself. A smile flitted across Edward Hearne's face, but he managed to suppress it before Irene saw it.

"Of course, of course. We'll get started right away," said Mr. Portman.

In those days, star touring companies had limited engagements. The local actors had to fill in the rest of the company and very quickly absorb lines and stage business in just the way the star demanded. Sometimes there was only one afternoon for rehearsal and local actors would have to memorize their lines in the wings right before they walked onstage. This is where the phrase "winging it" came from. Fortunately, we had almost three days to rehearse and I knew I would be grateful for every minute of it.

Mr. Portman led us onto the stage where a number of actors had already assembled. There were fifteen of us in all and everyone was either standing or sitting on chairs provided for that expressed purpose. It seemed so odd to me to be in the theater and view it from this perspective. I had never actually been on a stage before and now everything seemed so foreign—as if my world had suddenly been reversed. There was no scenery, no special lighting, and no one sat in the audience. It appeared barren and devoid of life. My theatrical experiences prior to this had been social occasions and packed houses. Now it seemed much too quiet and much too empty.

Mr. Portman broke into my reverie as he began to introduce us to one another, but was interrupted by Mrs. Davenport.

"I have a luncheon appointment and I do not want to be late. Shall we proceed as we did in Philadelphia two years ago?"

Although framed as a question, it really was more of a command. Mr. Portman quickly agreed, remarking how he knew that was just what Mr. Daly wanted.

Teddy stepped forward and, with the help of Bobby Martin, the call boy, double checked to make sure everyone was present.

It was Bobby's job to make us aware of time by warning us for our entrances and "calling us" when the time to appear on stage approached. He also ran errands and did odd jobs under the direction of the stage manager. Bobby was just thirteen, gangly, and at that awkward stage where he was constantly outgrowing his clothes. Right now, his pants weren't quite long enough.

He handed each of us in the cast the "sides," which were the pieces of dialogue each of the actors had in this version of the play. We were all expected to know the dialogue so well that we could figure what and where to come in. I was to be a supernumerary. In other words, whenever an extra female was needed, I was stage dressing. Animated and alive, but for all intents and purposes, I was really just part of the scenery.

Mr. Portman quickly explained our positions on the stage, which encompassed where we were to stand, enter and exit—the "blocking" of a scene. Essentially, for me, this meant staying out of the way of the main actors and never, never, upstaging Irene. I quickly learned that one did not want to get on the wrong side of Irene Davenport. Her anger was strong and her retribution was swift. Before our break for lunch, she'd already had two people fired.

And so began my introduction to the Scottish Play. This version was very different from the one I had pored over at

Grandmother's. This was Mrs. Davenport's personal version of the Bard's play. While there were a number of similarities, it was very much a Davenport production. A short dance had been added to ensure plenty of time for her to change costume, scenes had been rearranged, some cut out entirely and the part of Lady Macbeth had been enhanced. I had never been aware of these kinds of changes as an audience member; instead, I always became wrapped up in the performance. Now, I saw the differences.

The others assimilated this very quickly. I had problems with "stage directions" as they applied to movement. I thought of them from the point of view of the audience and in reality, stage right for instance was not the right side as the audience looked upon the stage, but as the actor looked out at them. I found this particularly confusing in reference to "up" and "down." Down was toward the audience, while up was away from the audience. It took some practice and Mary Cosgrove was very helpful in steering me in the correct direction until I got the hang of it.

It turned out to be a very long, very hot day. Even though my part was small, I was called upon to walk up and in over and over again. Mr. Portman paid agonizing attention to every detail. However, he was careful to move us in and around the main actors, making sure he didn't waste any of *their* time.

Irene complained about everything. She asked about the set pieces, what they would look like, why weren't they there yet. She argued with Mr. Hearne until he walked out and said he wouldn't return until she got control of herself. Mr. Portman trotted out after him and we all waited until he returned ten minutes later without Mr. Hearne. Mrs.

Davenport promptly said she, too, had had enough and left for her luncheon engagement.

The rest of us remained. We rehearsed the very few scenes without the two main actors and then, got our very welcome break for lunch.

That time away rejuvenated everyone. When Mr. Hearne and Mrs. Davenport returned, they were chillingly polite to one another. However, we were able to proceed. That afternoon, I got to rehearse my big scene in which I had one line:

"She has spoke what she should not, I am sure of that: Heaven knows what she has known."

This speech is part of Lady Macbeth's "mad scene," the final appearance in the play for Mrs. Davenport. I was so nervous that I almost missed my cue. Mr. Carlin, a very sweet elderly gentleman who played the Doctor, recited his line, and then looked at me encouragingly. Mary was in the scene with me, indeed, had all the rest of the Gentle-women's lines, and when she nudged me, I finally spoke my line. I was startled when Mr. Portman's voice yelled at me from the audience.

"You are going to have to speak up, much, much louder than that!"

I looked out into the audience, but it was just too dark to see anything. I had no idea anyone was out there. But, he was closely following the rehearsal. I repeated the line— stronger and louder and only received the approbation of "continue." Mrs. Davenport came on and I immediately backed away or moved "stage right," having learned that you must immediately give up the stage to the star and never, never, never upstage him or, in this case, her. This incredible faux pas occurs when you maneuver yourself toward the back of the stage and then, do or say something that requires the main actor to turn their back on the audience to look at or address you. I had been told that many a budding career had been terminated by that fatal mistake!

As soon as that scene was finished, Mrs. Davenport just walked out. Her dresser, Beatrice O'Neill, handed Irene her gloves and purse, she pulled on the gloves, nodded at Teddy and walked briskly toward the stage door exit. Bobby rushed to open the door for her and the only way I can describe her exit is that it was grand. She was gone without another word.

Nothing was like I had expected. We finished our rehearsal and people parted very quickly. Teddy handed me a sheet on which was a list of times that I was expected to be at the theater. It also indicated which dressing room would be mine, which I was to share with all the other women in the play.

I walked out the stage door I had come in and paused as it slammed shut behind me. I stood in the empty alley for a moment and thought about what I had just done and a feeling of immense satisfaction came over me. I felt as if I just experienced one of the premier events of my life. I had been ignored and disregarded and should have felt discouraged. Instead, as I stood in that alley outside the stage door, I felt empowered. That was the optimism of youth—I felt like I was on my way! As events proceeded, I needed that sense of empowerment more than I could have imagined.

Opening night was just two days away.

'Twas a rough night.

Macbeth Act II, Scene 3

∽∾∽∾∽∾∽∾∽∾∽∾∽∾∽∾∽∾∽∾∽∾∽∾∽∾∽∾∽

CHAPTER FOUR

I have become cognizant over the years that one should always approach a production of the Scottish Play with extreme caution. It is a play steeped in the supernatural, includes characters such as witches of the most evil kind, depicts the heinous crime of regicide and the most foul and unpleasant results of unbridled ambition. Death and the supernatural permeate the play. It is possible to become enmeshed in the metaphysical horror of it all and, if one allows it, the play can create a sense of unease in one's own mind. And, as most theater people know, the play itself is cursed.

There are some who say the curse goes all the way back to 1606 and the first production for King James. In America, the curse on this play started in 1849 with the Astor Place Riot. At that time there was an intense professional rivalry between the famous American actor Edwin Forrest, (after whom my favorite actor, Edwin Booth, was named) and an equally famous English actor, William Charles Macready. In May of 1849, Macready was completing a farewell tour of the United States and he attempted to perform the main role in the Scottish Play. I say attempted because Forrest's fans, of which there were legions, howled down Macready during a performance in New York at the Astor Place Opera House.

Macready continued to perform, convinced of his safety by the more polite and aristocratic elements of New York society. On May 10, his performance went off without incident inside the theater—but outside, an angry mob of somewhere between ten and fifteen thousand people had formed in protest. They began to stone the theater. The infantry was called out, emotions flared and eventually, the order to fire on the crowd was given. When the dust cleared, over twenty people were dead.

Macready left the country in disguise and never returned. It was a scandal and major tragedy that followed both Edwin Forrest and William Charles Macready the rest of their lives.

What became known as the Astor Place Riot went down in American theatrical history and is now the stuff of legend. It has a special place in my emotions, not only because it is directly associated with the play in which I first appeared onstage as an actress, but also because Macready later became known for the assistance and inspiration he gave to an American actress who eventually became the great Charlotte Cushman. As you know, she was my inspiration when I was just twelve.

Since 1849, other productions of the play were performed where people were hurt—in one case, an actor playing Macduff received a wound during a stage fight that eventually resulted in his death. And, of course, what happened to Irene Davenport is part of the myth and legend, as well. All this is attributed to the play itself, which is why one never speaks the title of the Scottish Play unless one is required to do so while onstage during a production.

All this I learned much later, but I share it with you now. Because, dear Agnes, my sincere advice to you is, as you set about your career, take particular care when approaching this specific play of Mr. Shakespeare and diligently follow the prescribed rules!

Once again, I digress.

On opening night, I found myself overwhelmed with excitement. For three days, I had been introduced and initiated into the life and rhythm of theater on the other side of the curtain. Now, I would be introduced to what that would be like in front of an audience. The performance was sold out and rumor had it there were many famous and important Chicago personages in the audience. Mr. Portman told me in confidence that for some reason, Irene had never performed in Chicago and so the audience flocked to see her in what was considered her debut.

My only disappointment was that none of my family save Grandmother was coming to see me. John William had managed to smuggle a note to me through Grandmother telling me how angry our parents were, but how proud he was of me for proceeding. I still have that correspondence and when I get very low, I re-read it and it always makes me feel better. Amazingly enough, James Jr. sent a small arrangement of flowers and when I saw them, I was really touched by how kind the gesture was until I opened the card.

> *These flowers are a token of my trust that this experience will show you the error of your ways, that you will quickly come to your senses, return home and embrace your proper future.*
>
> *Regards,*
>
> *JJ*

My feelings of appreciation for his kindness quickly evaporated.

I wish I could remember every detail of that performance. I simply cannot. What I do remember is how awkwardly I thought everything was proceeding. People were late for cues. Props were missing or showed up right before they were required. And it was so very hot. My dress stuck to me. I couldn't help but notice that as the night wore on Mr. Hearne drank heavily from a particular water pitcher that was set on the prop table and made available for his exclusive use. Several times, I watched as he came off stage and poured himself a glass and drank it down. The heat must have made him incredibly thirsty.

I was so engrossed in watching the whole experience from backstage that I almost missed my cue for the introduction to the mad scene. It was the pinnacle scene for Mrs. Davenport—the sleepwalking scene for Lady Macbeth—and the only scene in which I had a line.

I found myself on the wrong side of the stage. Once again, I had confused "stage right" with "stage left." I saw Mary on the correct side standing in the wings, gesturing for me. My heart sank as I heard the orchestra take up the introduction of the tenor for the *entr'acte* and I watched as he took his place center stage. The curtain opened and, as he began to sing, I became frantic with the need to get over to where Mary was in time for our entrance. I considered my options. I could wait and rush across the stage after the curtain closed when he was finished, which would mean that I would have to pass by Mrs. Davenport (and probably end my very short-lived career) or find my way behind the scenery in the dark, hoping not to be seen. I took what I determined to be the safest course: I would pick my way through the scenery and, hopefully, get onto the correct side of the stage in plenty of time.

Very carefully, I began to creep across the back of the set, but it was so very dark. I ran smack dab into the flat for Act Three and it began to sway. I reached out and grabbed it—who knows what it must have looked like during the *entr'acte*! I decided I could go no further and had to retrace my steps. I would have to rush across the stage after the curtain closed.

That is how I ended up on the wrong side of the stage just before the scene started in which Irene Davenport died.

My heart beat fast and I was in agony, knowing that I wasn't in the right place at the right time. I did manage to keep my wits about me. It was only when Irene appeared before me that I began to feel really uncomfortable. I knew she was getting ready to say something truly awful to me when, at that moment, the *entr'acte* ended and the curtain closed. I ran for it, passing the tenor, Harold Jordan as he exited stage right, stopping only when I stood breathless next to Mary. I looked back across the stage, but the only

thing I could see was the face of Irene Davenport, illuminated by the light of the single white candle she held in her
hand.

She stared at me and her face was contorted in anger,
but I looked away, stepped onstage with Mary and, when it
was my turn, said my line clearly and loudly. However, it
was all for naught because it was completely drowned out
by the overwhelming response of the audience to the
entrance of Irene as the mad Lady Macbeth.

Those moments passed by quickly as I watched,
enraptured. This was nothing like the rehearsals. She
performed magnificently and my whole attention was still
focused upon her. It became apparent that no one in the
audience cared if we were there or not. Slowly, I became
unaware of anyone else around me, so focused was I on
Irene. I had never seen a performance that up close and was
completely absorbed in the power of it. There was no break
until she was done and then, a huge pause. It was if the
entire audience had been holding their collective breaths.
You could feel the silence and then, the exhale as every
person in the theater was on his or her feet calling and
shouting. There was Irene taking it all in, bowing, absorbing
every accolade, looking humble, but taking it all in as if it
were her due.

Mr. Carlin gestured to us, and I stepped back into the
shadows and faded away so that Irene would have the
stage to herself. It was obvious that no one in the audience
was interested in listening to a word we said.

I stood in the wings and slowly became conscious of
people standing, moving around me. Irene was onstage
taking her bows. Bobby ran past me and onto the stage, a

huge bouquet of yellow roses in his arms. He gave them to Irene and quickly exited on the other side. Then, technicians began to ready the next scene and I just stood listening to the thunderous applause.

I heard Teddy Ryan's voice hiss, "What the hell is going on with that curtain?"

I became aware of the movement of the heavy velvet act curtain. And then, I saw the large, painted flats begin to move skyward into the fly space of the theater's roof.

So, that's where they go.

My attention momentarily shifted upward as I watched the movement of the scenery. Suddenly a scream pierced the auditorium and it immediately drew my notice back onto the stage.

It was the most amazing thing. Irene seemed to be attached to one of the pieces of scenery that was rising into the fly space. I wondered at first, as your mind does at times like this, if this were some new strange part of the play that we hadn't rehearsed.

In the house the applause had stopped, replaced by the noise and confusion of hundreds of people straining to get out of the building—there was practically a stampede to get out of the theater. I was aware of all that as if it were happening in the background as I could not take my eyes off Irene.

"Cut the rope!" I heard Teddy scream. "Cut the damn rope, for the love of God, cut the rope!"

Irene's hands were on her throat. As she tugged at her pearls, her face became twisted and ugly. She was gasping for breath and making the most awful sounds. It was horrible.

Teddy's scream was echoed by one of a group of gentlemen from the audience who had appeared on stage. And then, suddenly, the scenery crashed to the floor of the stage and with it the inert form of Irene Davenport. She hit the stage with a terrible impact and it was then that I looked away.

Bobby Martin almost immediately came up to me and I stared at him, as if I were seeing him for the first time. He had Mr. Hearne's pitcher in his hand and poured out some liquid in a glass and handed it to me. I took a sip, gasped and began coughing—it was alcohol! Mr. Hearne appeared and took the pitcher from Bobby, sent him away for some water and said something soothing about coming away with him. He put his arm around my shoulder and led me away, sat me on a chair out of sight of the stage and disappeared. I started to shake uncontrollably. It seemed only a moment later that Teddy found me, got me up and helped me downstairs to the women's dressing room. He left me in the hands of the other women in the production and ran back upstairs. All we could do was look at each other, the shock and dismay plain upon our faces. Still unable to stop shaking, I burst into tears. Mary found a shawl and wrapped it tightly around me. She sat down next to me and I buried my head in her shoulder and wept.

That was a very long time ago indeed, but the memory of the events that took place that evening call up emotions that can still overpower me. I am afraid I was always the sensitive one in the family—easily weeping over the death of a beloved pet, for instance. If one of my brothers hurt somehow in their play, I was never any good as a nurse, as I was prone to completely lose my composure and break into tears.

It seemed a very long time that I sat with Mary. Eventually, I stopped crying and my body became calm. Mary offered me a handkerchief and while I wiped my face, she changed out of her costume. She said that she was going back upstairs to see what was going on. Not wanting her to leave, I asked her to wait, changed out of my costume as quickly as I could and followed right behind. The backstage area had erupted into activity and my natural curiosity came to the forefront. I very carefully stayed out of sight of Irene's body, but I began to watch what was taking place around me. The first thing I became aware of was the fact that the audience was gone and the house had that feeling of emptiness and hollowness it only has when no one is "out there."

As they re-opened the main act curtain, two men dressed in formal attire, obvious theater patrons, passed by me and went out the back stage door. I got closer to the stage and it was then that Beatrice O'Neill pushed me aside and ran toward Irene Davenport's body. She was weeping hysterically. Her dark clothes had blended into the darkness and the shadows of the backstage area. She appeared as if by magic, startling those around her.

"What happened to my lady? Where is she? Let me see her!"

She ran over toward the stage and, once again, Teddy was there and he grabbed her.

"You don't want to see her now, Beatrice. Let her be."

O'Neill promptly fainted. Teddy sighed, lifted her inert body up as if it weighed hardly anything, carried her off the stage and laid her on a cot in his office.

Suddenly, the oddest sensation came over me. I became cold, bone-chillingly, physically cold. I looked at my arm and could see goose bumps. My mind told me how odd this was, as it had been stifling hot only a moment before. I don't know how much time passed. It could have been minutes, it could have been hours, but I remember looking up to find Teddy Ryan at my side. He spoke my name and it seemed as if I was hearing him from a long way off. His voice was soft and kind, but carried a sense of urgency. I suddenly remembered he was addressing me, calling me Miss Nolan and that was my name.

"They are going to take her out now, Miss Nolan. Your grandmother is here to take you home."

Behind him stood the person in my life who had always been my rock, my refuge.

"Rosemary, it's time to go," Grandmother said.

Teddy guided me over to her and I stepped into the embrace of that dear woman. At that moment, I knew it was going to be all right. The coldness quickly dissipated and I began to feel warm again.

"She's probably overwhelmed," he told her. "Best to take her home now. I'll take care of everything here."

Grandmother smiled at him and said, "Thank you, Teddy."

We walked out, Grandmother's arm on my shoulder, and just as we opened the back stage door, a young man rushed in. He was dressed in a business suit and he pushed past us, grabbed Teddy by the collar and pulled him close.

"What the hell happened? Where is Bobby?" he yelled.

I had to turn around and look. Even in my distress, it registered that this was the most handsome man I had ever seen. He was large and broad-shouldered with dark hair and brilliant blue eyes. I felt my heart leap in my chest. If there is such a thing as love at very first sight, I believed that, in that moment, I was in the grip of it. He was in his early twenties and there was a sense of maturity about him that I found strangely compelling. I could not stop staring at him.

Grandmother was totally unaware of my reaction. She dropped my arm and the coachman helped her into the carriage, which was parked at the end of the alley. I remained staring off after the young man talking with Teddy Ryan. He never looked back at me, never even noticed I was there. Grandmother's coachman came forward.

"Miss, your grandmother is waiting."

In a daze, I turned and he led me over to the carriage and helped me in. I settled down next to Grandmother and, after that, I don't remember what happened next because it was at that point that I just seemed to shut down. It was only the next morning when I woke to the late September sunlight that I realized Irene Davenport was truly dead and I had seen it happen. The young man I had seen also seemed as if he had been part of a dream I'd had.

All these memories crowd through my mind now, as I think back about those terrible moments when I stood in the wings and watched Irene Davenport twist and gasp and die. Agnes, my dear, I'm sure you must think that any normal girl would have left the theater that night and never returned. But, not even that event—as horrible as it was—could end my interest in a theatrical life or lessen my resolve to be an actress. It did impact it. Oh yes, it inexorably changed my life forever and in ways that I could not possibly predict, or at that time, even imagine. As events were about to unfold, it propelled me forward into the role of the protagonist in a drama that was to reveal her murderer.

But, once again, I get ahead of myself.

Nothing in his life
Became him like the leaving it...

Macbeth Act I, Scene 4

~~~~~~

CHAPTER FIVE

Over the course of my long life in the theater, I have come to the realization that if one chooses this path, one will come to live two lives simultaneously. One life is your own, your *personal* life. The life where you know who you are, where you came from, who your friends are, and who your family is. The other is your life in the theater. Your theatrical life belongs to the characters that you take on, what the audience sees, and what you live every night and every matinee. And when that is over, that life is also over, including all of the relationships you made with the cast members during the run of that particular production. Sometimes, you meet them again and renew the relationship; but if you never meet them again, the acquaintanceship ceases to exist.

For some actors, the two lives are completely different and separate as they are able to compartmentalize their thoughts and feelings. For others, there is no difference at all and the two meld so closely as to be as one. For me, they would always be separate, not mutually exclusive. But, I know I will never forget, nor purge from my being, the part of my person that sprang to life the night the Great Irene Davenport died. A kaleidoscope of visions flooded my brain and it came as no surprise to me or indeed to anyone who knew me well, that I was mesmerized by the idea of Irene Davenport as she lay on the floor, a cordon of people surrounding her. If that sight was quite gruesome, then the funeral for Irene was quite spectacular.

The next morning, I awoke in the bedroom that Grandmother had allowed me to claim as my own. I had no idea what time it was, but the sun was well up. I felt lethargic, drained, and when my door opened a crack and then closed, I knew it was past time to get up and get on with my day. A moment later, Grandmother entered.

"Well, you certainly suffered a shock last night."

"Oh, Grandmother, it was the most amazing evening," I cried.

"It was indeed that! I took the liberty of asking Doctor Sanderson to stop by this morning," Grandmother said. "He only said that you had had a severe shock and you should be allowed to sleep as long as possible. He told me that you would awake in due course and so you have. How are you feeling?"

"Well enough, I suppose...considering."

She smiled and I smiled back—we always understood each other.

"You haven't had a bite to eat since yesterday afternoon. Cook's sending up a tray. Thank God you're young; you'll spring back from this."

"May I see the papers?"

"Of course—what a stir it has caused."

As I ate, I looked over the *Times*, the *Tribune* and the *Journal*, which were all spread out upon my bed. The spectacular method of Irene's death was first page news. It had pushed just about everything else to the back of every paper. Of course, the police had been called in, even the Chief Fire Marshall, Robert A. Williams, had appeared at the theater because someone had thought to ring in the call from one of the nearby alarm boxes spread across the city, reporting the matter erroneously as a fire. He was quoted as saying how serious a matter it was. With the drought, resources were spread thin and the fire department couldn't be responding to false alarms.

Over and over again, Irene's beauty and talent was acclaimed. It was widely agreed that her performance had enraptured the audience and was perhaps the greatest of her career. One paper had even managed to obtain commentaries from other well-known actors and producers with whom she had performed like Dion Boucicault who had telegrammed, "A light unlike any other has been extinguished through this terrible tragedy." Of course, Mr. Daly was also quoted as saying, "Irene Davenport was a magnificent actress. Her talent and stamina for tragedienne roles was legendary."

I read every word. When the police were asked for comment, they only remarked that a very thorough investigation had been done and no foul play was suspected. It appeared to all and sundry that what happened to Irene was a very tragic and unfortunate accident and all witnesses agreed. Of course, there were over twenty-six hundred of them and I couldn't imagine that they contacted and spoke with every one. At that time, I just assumed like everyone else that it was a horrible, horrible accident.

This morning, with light streaming into my bedroom, what I had witnessed the night before seemed more of a dream than reality. Reading about it in the black and white of the newspapers removed it from my personal frame of reference and made it appear like something that happened to someone else. I wondered what was going to happen next. Was my career over after one night? Would Mr. Daly close the play? Who could possibly replace Irene? Even that was addressed in the papers, as several of them noted that Mr. Andrew Portman had received a telegram from Mr. Daly and the content of it was quoted in its entirety:

> I am devastated by the death of Irene Davenport.
> The theatrical world has lost a great talent. Play
> closed for three days while we mourn the death of
> our beloved actress.

I was surprised at the depth of Mr. Daly's emotion. It seemed to me to be pure hyperbole. Irene was well respected, admired even, but it was difficult for me to imagine her as "beloved."

The papers all speculated that we might just be privileged to see some other great actress in the role of Lady Macbeth and several well-known names were mentioned. Due to the heat, the funeral was to take place tomorrow at

Crosby's Opera House. She was going to be buried in Chicago!

Crosby's Opera House had been shut down for renovation for the past several months and was due to re-open on the ninth of October with a ten-day series of concerts performed by the well-known Theodore Thomas Orchestra. It was almost completed, and since no performances were scheduled until then, it was available for Irene's funeral. Mr. Daly must have used his connections to arrange it.

As I read about the funeral plans, Grandmother came into my bedroom to tell me I had a visitor. She advised me to get dressed and come downstairs as soon as possible.

When I got downstairs, Bobby Martin was standing in the front parlor. I knew he did not feel quite comfortable and I could tell he was very nervous. But, as Grandmother was always the consummate hostess and knew very well the needs of growing boys, she had placed a plate of sugar cookies and a pitcher of lemonade on the mahogany serving table.

I smiled at him.

"Oh, Miss Nolan," he said. "Mr. Ryan said to tell everyone there's a meeting this afternoon at the theater. Three p.m. sharp."

"How are you feeling, Bobby? I think we're all under shock."

There was pain in his eyes.

So, I just said, "Yes, I saw that you had just given her those flowers."

"I didn't know they was unlucky. Got reamed out for it, but it wasn't my fault," he cried.

"Of course, not. Here sit down," I said.

I got him to perch at the end of Grandmother's rose damask sofa.

"Would you like some lemonade?"

I handed him a glass and he took a sip.

"Miss Nolan, you have to believe it wasn't my fault."

"Of course not, Bobby. Try a cookie."

He bit into one and the expression on his face showed me that he didn't very often get a treat like that.

"Why would anyone think you had anything to do with her accident?" I asked.

"I gave her the yellow flowers. Teddy—Mr. Ryan says yellow is bad luck in the theater."

"Maybe so, but you got the flowers from someone else, didn't you?"

"They was sitting on a box by the stage door. It's my job to check for deliveries. We knew there was going to be a lot of flowers. You should see backstage now—it's a regular funeral parlor."

His face flushed at that. "I didn't mean…"

"Of course you didn't. Was there a note with the flowers you found last night?"

"Yes, but I can't—I didn't read it. You know how she is—was. I had to make sure she got them as soon as possible. I didn't know about the color."

"Well, that certainly wasn't the cause of her death."

"Yeah. That's what the police said, too."

All of a sudden, he jumped up.

"Well, thanks for the cookies."

"Take another—take some with you."

"Thanks, I will."

In that moment, he looked so young, more like my brother, Francis. I realized that they must be about the same age. I wondered about the boy in front of me. Where were his parents and why did he need to work for a living? I realized that he must be in fear of the loss of his job. I couldn't resist asking him about his family.

"Are you alone, Bobby? I mean, have you any parents?"

"Oh, Miss, they're long gone. My mom died when I was two and my dad's been gone for years. It's just me and my brother."

"You have a brother?"

"Ooh, yes, he was there last night, too. Well, have to go, have five more people and the meeting is soon. I'll tell Mr. Ryan you'll be there."

"Oh, absolutely. And thank you, Bobby, for coming to tell me."

He stuffed one more cookie in his mouth and he was out the door and gone.

That afternoon, Teddy seemed very thoughtful and preoccupied when I walked through the stage door. He did ask me if I was all right when he checked my name off of a list. He seemed satisfied with my answer that I had recovered as well as could be expected and pointed to a large chalk board that had been set up. Mr. Portman had written a message that we would be meeting in the Green Room. Thank goodness it wasn't to be onstage.

I peeked in on the stage and noticed it had been completely swept clean—no evidence of last night's events remained. Instead, it was quite orderly. The only thing unusual was the piece of scenery still askew: a large flat lay on its side, a rope dangled from above, but that would mostly likely be fixed later.

As I walked downstairs to the area under the stage and passed along the corridor where the dressing rooms were, I saw Edward Hearne standing outside his dressing room talking with Bobby Martin. He laughed and tousled Bobby's hair and then, gave him an affectionate pat on the shoulder. He leaned over and whispered something in Bobby's ear. Bobby took a step back away from Edward, but then Edward pulled a coin from his pocket and held it out to Bobby. When Bobby saw the money, his eyes lit up and he smiled. Edward handed him the coin and I heard him say, "There's a good boy, now, off you go."

Bobby nodded to Edward, turned, and ran down the corridor and out of the scenery load-in door, which exited off of Monroe Street. Mr. Hearne pivoted and moved on down toward the Green Room. In his most elegant voice he spoke the last line of the play.

"…by the grace of Grace

We will perform in measure, time, and place:

So, thanks to all at once and to each one–"

Mr. Ryan called out sharply, "Mr. Hearne!"

Edward stopped immediately.

"I do apologize, Mr. Ryan. For a moment, I forgot where I was," Edward said.

"I should think so, Mr. Hearne. I am thinking we don't need any more bad luck than we have already had," Teddy said and continued on down the corridor.

Mr. Hearne turned to me and I asked him, "What was that about?"

"I am sure you ascertain from Mr. Ryan's reaction that quoting the last line of the play when not onstage performing it is very bad," he said, with a twinkle in his eye.

"Is it?" I asked.

"Oh, most assuredly. May I escort you?" He offered me his arm and we proceeded to the Green Room together.

The term Green Room is, in fact, a misnomer. Every theater has one and very rarely is the Green Room actually green. Rather, it is considered a room of rest or a room of convenience where an actor can wait until called upon to perform onstage. Sometimes, actors gather during or after a performance to relax or converse with one another.

The Green Room at the Grand was decorated in accordance with the rest of the design of the theater—in blue and gold. It had several divans and a number of comfortable side chairs. Theatrical handbills that featured famous actors and actresses had been framed and lined the walls. There were bookshelves and tables filled with the latest newspapers and theatrical periodicals. I had been in this room only once before when I had peeked in after finding my dressing room on the first day of rehearsals. It was hard to believe that only four days had passed.

As I looked over those in attendance, the lighter mood engendered by Mr. Hearne's presence started to fade. It was a very solemn group that met that afternoon. I realized over the short time I had worked with them that the only person who I felt I knew at all was Mary Cosgrove and she smiled warmly at me. I had so completely focused on learning what I had to know that I had not spent any time getting to know the rest of the people in the production.

The entire cast was there, as well as Mrs. Davenport's dresser, Mrs. Beatrice O'Neil, who seemed to be the only one in any real distress. She was a tall and spare woman, plain and pale. It was obvious from her countenance that she hadn't slept well last night or at all, for that matter. Dressed entirely and unremittingly in black, she held a white handkerchief in her hands and only stopped twisting it to use it to dab her eyes. Her pain of loss certainly was heartfelt. I suddenly recalled her collapse last night on seeing Irene's body. I understood that she had been with Mrs. Davenport for a very long time.

Mary saved me a seat and I quickly sat down next to her. Even her blonde vivaciousness was subdued today. Edward Hearne sat across the room from us and reached for the pitcher, which I now knew did not contain water, and poured a drink. People were speaking quietly with one another in subdued tones as I looked around the room. The gentle Joseph Carlin, who performed the role of the Doctor and appeared in my big scene, as well as several other minor roles, sat to my left. Next to him sat the aristocratic Miriam Simmons who portrayed Lady Macduff. Across from her, standing behind one of the divans, paced the athletic, but gruff Alan Kelly, who had the role of Macduff. I spotted the three women who portrayed the three witches—Alice Alstairs, Gertrude Manton, and Ruth Fountain—sitting together on a large divan, behind which Alan Kelly continued to pace. I realized I had not talked to any of them at all. Irene was the only one missing and somehow, it was her presence that I felt most strongly, perhaps because we had all assembled solely due to her absence.

Mr. Portman walked into the room. Immediately, conversations ended in mid-sentence and all eyes turned to Mr. Daly's representative. Today, his suit was an appropriate dark grey and there was a black arm band on his upper left arm. His black hair stood out starkly against his paler than usual face. There were bags under his eyes and he looked like he hadn't had any sleep. His manner was much harried and I knew he was dealing with events well beyond his expectations.

"Good afternoon, everyone. Thank you for coming. This is an exceptionally difficult time."

Mr. Hearne spoke up.

"Andrew, I think it would go a long way to easing the minds of many of us here if you could let us know what is going to happen to the play," he said.

There was a murmur of assent throughout the assembled group. It suddenly occurred to me that the morose mood was not so much connected to Irene and what had happened to her as it was with their concern over the future of their employment.

"In good time, Hearne," Mr. Portman said. "First of all, Mr. Daly sends his condolences to all of us who knew and loved Irene Davenport."

There was a pause, during which no one added any commentary. A few of the actors even looked away, so Mr. Portman continued.

"He wants to let the cast know that he has no intentions, at this time, of closing the production."

There was an almost audible release of tension and the anxiety level in the room, which had been very high, fell considerably.

"However, he is in the process of finding and contacting other premier actresses suitable for the challenge of the role of Lady Macbeth who are available for the tour. So far, there has been some reluctance on the part of the women he has spoken with to step into, as it were, Irene's shoes. He thinks until an appropriate person has been found, he wants to consider utilizing the talents of the understudy. He feels Mr. Hearne is a big enough star–" Here, Mr. Hearne bowed his head, "and Macbeth a big enough role to carry the show."

Everyone turned to Mary. She was the assigned understudy for Irene. In all honesty, she was an understudy nobody had ever expected—including Mary—to be utilized. Her eyes opened very wide and their green color seemed to intensify, but she remained speechless.

"However, in light of the tragedy and subsequent publicity, he wants every female actress within range to audition."

There was an audible gasp from several of the group—including myself. Me? Audition for Lady Macbeth? I couldn't do it! Could I? What if I could?

Mr. Hearne spoke up with more than a touch of sarcasm.

"I see publicity is the optimal word here! Isn't Augustin concerned it will turn against him?"

"Mr. Hearne, I think you know Mr. Daly well enough to know that he can handle the press," Mr. Portman replied. "We all know what an expensive proposition this tour is; there is a considerable sum of money at stake. Whether we use this theater or not, leases have been signed, contracts have been agreed to and it is important that we do not close the show. We must have an audience here until he is able to attract a name for the role of Lady Macbeth. And, therefore, any publicity is good publicity. I think we can agree that not one of us wants to be put in the position of seeking new employment at the beginning of the season."

Mr. Hearne merely nodded.

"I'm here to tell you, auditions will commence promptly at eleven o'clock tomorrow morning."

"But, tomorrow is the funeral, man. What about paying our respects to Irene? What are the plans for that?" Allan Kelly asked.

"Oh, yes, you're absolutely correct, Mr. Kelly. The funeral is set for ten-thirty and I have made arrangements for seating for each one of you. Please be at the Crosby Opera House no later than ten, as we are expecting many important personages from the Chicago community, even the mayor, the honorable Roswell B. Mason, has agreed to attend."

Around the room people nodded their heads, but they were not a happy group. It appeared that no one was comfortable with these arrangements.

It was Miriam Simmons who finally voiced what everyone was thinking.

"It is certainly better than closing the play and throwing us all out of work, but the timing is certainly less than optimal–"

Mr. Portman shook his head.

"I know how it looks, but time is of the essence. Mr. Daly will close the theater for three days to show respect for Irene, so that means we must choose a new Lady Macbeth tomorrow, have one day of rehearsal, and open on Wednesday night. Are there any questions?"

"What if we don't want to audition?" Gertrude Manton, who portrayed the First Witch, asked.

"You are not required to and if you do not appear promptly—let us say at five o'clock tomorrow afternoon—we will assume that you do not wish to be considered. Oh, and I will require Mr. Hearne to be here, as well, to read with the ladies. Anything else?"

There was no response except for a sniff from Beatrice O'Neill.

"Thank you all for coming. I will see you all tomorrow morning. Mr. Hearne, ladies, I will plan to see you onstage here at five tomorrow afternoon."

As the group broke up, I asked Mr. Portman who was going to make the final decision on casting the role of Lady Macbeth.

"Mr. Daly, of course. He is on his way here from New York, as we speak."

That night, I couldn't sleep at all. I was so excited about the prospect of auditioning for the great Augustin Daly. I walked around as if I were in a trance. I couldn't believe it. Of course, I knew it was likely that Miriam Simmons would have the role—she was so much older. But, I thought it was really Mary Cosgrove who should get it. She was the understudy, and she had so much more experience than I. But, to have the chance to audition…it was a dream come true. It meant that my acting career wasn't over! It meant there was hope. At least the play would go on and that was good. But, even better, I could make a connection with Mr. Daly, perhaps even an *impression* upon him! I immersed myself in every scene in which Lady Macbeth appeared. I must have driven even my patient Grandmother mad with my recitations.

The only interruption came the next morning, when it was time to attend the funeral. As a member of the cast, I sat near the front of what turned out to be a very crowded event. Crosby's Opera House was a magnificent setting for this last tribute to Irene.

As an actress, there was some controversy over the fact that Irene simply could not be buried at a church. Even today, actresses do not enjoy the best of reputations, although we have come a long way in that regard even though certain film actresses do not often help that image. But, this is 1951. In 1871, things were very different. Actresses had the worst of reputations— whether true or not, did not matter—and often, were considered adulteresses or worse. Many fine actresses— including myself—worked very hard to change that image, but it was firmly entrenched in the minds of the public. For Irene Davenport, however, there was no possibility of a church funeral. It had to be in the theater. It couldn't be in the Grand, either. Can you imagine? Eulogized on the very stage on which she had died? Sensational, but over the boundaries of good taste. Instead, Mr. Daly had arranged for the use of Crosby's Opera House.

The next day, Grandmother and I—for there was no way Grandmother was going to miss the event—made our way to Crosby's Opera House. We joined a line of carriages waiting to drop off those attending the funeral. The street was lined with onlookers, as well.

Inside, we made our way to the reserved seats and took our places. Irene's coffin was arranged onstage and backed by some of the most beautiful flowers I had ever seen. There was a huge spray of white lilies across the top of the casket and two large standards on either side. Banked in front were floral arrangements from theatrical luminaries from across the country. As I sat in the first row, the heady perfume from the flowers was almost overpowering. It felt as if I sat in the middle of a conservatory.

The house was filled to capacity. It seemed as if every theater person who happened to be appearing in Chicago at that time was in attendance. I recognized the famous actors Joseph Jefferson III and Lawrence Barrett, and the well-known producer, Lester Wallack, all suitably clothed for mourning and sitting in the orchestra section. There were many in attendance I did not know at that time—actors, producers, designers and technicians—but whom I would come to know in the following years. Our group, as members of the last company of players with whom Irene had performed, was seated together. I became conscious of the many eyes upon us. It was an eerie feeling and not very pleasant at all.

The service itself was not overly long. There was no clergyman. Mary confided in me that Mr. Daly could not get one to agree to come. They were all so concerned about their own reputations. They could not risk being seen at the funeral service of an actress, particularly one who had been so famous and had died in such spectacular fashion. So, Mr. Daly himself took on this position and really created quite a spectacle.

It was, bar none, the best funeral I've ever attended (and I'm at an age where I have attended more than I would care to count)—certainly the best ever produced. The orchestra played "Rock of Ages" and "Abide with Me"—two of my favorite hymns and performed them very beautifully.

Mr. Daly sat on the stage. When it came time for him to speak, he stood and walked to a podium that had been set up for him. A tall man, full-figured with a neat mustache, he was well-dressed in his mourning clothes. He looked tired after his journey from New York and the stress of recent events. He must have boarded a train the minute he got the word about Irene's death in order to be here so promptly. He spoke eloquently of his long association with and appreciation for Mrs. Davenport. He praised her great talent and said how the theatrical world had suffered a great loss. His respect for actresses was well known and he would eventually write a book which was a tribute to actresses. He called up Mr. Hearne, who was prepared with a very nice, albeit short, eulogy, which he delivered in his rich and powerful voice.

We were out of the theater by noon and, as we stood outside, the carriages quickly filled and dispersed. There was a stand of trees across the street from where we stood and many of the leaves were wilted and had turned brown. They were not the vibrant brown color of fall, but the result of every living thing shrinking and dying from the lack of water. I could not help that they seemed to express the dryness in the atmosphere of putting Irene Davenport to her eternal rest, as well.

Not many chose to go to the cemetery, but Grandmother wanted to go. As we stepped out of our coach,

Grandmother suddenly exclaimed, "Well, so the rumors were true!"

"What rumors, Grandmother?"

She nodded in the direction away from the crowd. There were two men I had never seen before who were obviously not theater people. The two of them stood and waited as the hearse pulled up to the cemetery. Then, I realized that I did recognize one, only because of the dark suit he wore. He had been in formal wear the night Irene died and I had seen him onstage after she fell. He was the older of the two and, as he watched her casket being carried toward the gravesite by the pallbearers, he bowed his head.

"Who are they?" I asked.

"The older one is Samuel Connelly. The younger is his right hand man, Paul Coopersmith. "

She said this as if I should know exactly who they were. I looked at her blankly. She sighed.

"He's a very successful Chicago business owner," she continued. "He built his fortune in lumber. Some say he is a millionaire. He is one of your father's wealthiest clients, even more so than the Waldens."

"I don't believe Father ever had him over to the house."

"Of course not. He is an exceptionally private man, a widower. But, you know, now that I recall, I saw him with Irene Davenport at a restaurant during my last theater trip to New York. There was some talk that he planned to marry her."

I looked at her in absolute amazement. Had Irene Davenport been planning to give up her career in the theater when she died? Grandmother guessed my thoughts.

"Of course, you cannot understand that. You are just beginning, but Irene Davenport did not have too many more years left as a premier leading lady. While she was at the height of her fame, she probably knew that it would not last. Perhaps she was planning her next career move."

Grandmother was a shrewd judge of character, but the idea that Irene Davenport would ever give up her career, her fame, was unthinkable to me. I could only nod.

Once we arrived at the gravesite, my attention was directed towards observing what was going on around me. This was my very first funeral and it was filled with curiosity seekers. Standing on a small hill, trying to catch a bit of shade in the cemetery, I realized there was no one who truly cared about Irene, merely those who were there out of curiosity or requirement. It was then that I noticed Mrs. O'Neill, her face wet with tears. It appeared as if only she had cared for Irene. They had most likely grown close, Mrs. O'Neill having taken care of all her personal needs for so long. I watched as she walked over to the casket and placed a red rose on the top. As I looked around, I noticed that every other face was completely dry.

And then, I saw Mr. Connelly walk over to Mrs. O'Neill and attempt to speak with her. She turned abruptly away from him and moved toward the waiting coaches that Mr. Daly had provided. I turned my attention back and then, seemingly out of nowhere, my eyes were captured by the visage of the same young gentleman who arrived just as I was leaving the theater the night Irene died. My heart did a flip as I observed him standing right next to Mary Cosgrove. Much taller than she, he had to bend over in order to say something to her. She stiffened and looked up into his face. Her whole demeanor changed and, for a split second, I could see her body go rigid with anger. He said something else and she appeared to relax. She lightly touched his arm and turned away from him.

Who is he?

Grandmother tapped my arm and indicated, with a nod of her head, where Mr. Daly stood by Irene's open grave. I saw him take some notes out of his pocket. He said a few well-chosen and rehearsed words. The whole thing struck me as rather impersonal and unremittingly sad. Fortunately, it was over quickly. Everyone dispersed almost immediately after that. I desperately wanted to go over to Mary and be introduced to her friend, but I did not get a chance, as Grandmother took out a black lace fan and started waving it back and forth.

"Let's go home, dear. I believe I've had enough for one day."

When we arrived back home, Grandmother insisted we both lay down for a while. I had not intended to take a nap before the audition. I was so keyed up, but a tremendous lethargy overcame me and it seemed as if I could barely make it up the stairs to my room. I walked over to the bed, laid upon it and immediately fell into a deep, dark sleep.

I dreamt about Irene. As I lay sleeping, I fell into so deep a state of unconsciousness that it was almost like a form of paralysis, for I felt as if I could not move a single muscle. I looked up and there she was, floating above me. She was as I had seen her last at the theater, but there was such a look of fierce intensity upon her face that it scared me. She was whispering, but I could not make out what she said.

Fear coursed through every vein in my body. The dream was so real; I felt as if I could have touched her, for she was complete in every detail and appeared whole and alive. I desperately wanted to scream, but not a sound emerged from my throat. I could not move at all and I felt helpless, a prisoner of the spirit of Irene Davenport. It was not possible to look away. I wanted to wake up, but was unable to do that either. My mind screamed *it is only a dream, only a dream*, but I could not speak and could not awaken.

Then, I heard her say, in the softest breath, *murder*. My entire body went cold, but still I could not awaken. She seemed to drift above me and then over to my right side and there she stood and remained by my bedside. She whispered again.

You must avenge me.

The effort seemed to cost her a great deal and she became less clear until she was completely gone and I found myself wide-awake. I could move once again, but still had little control. My entire body began to shake. I sat up and wrapped my arms about myself and began to rock back and forth. A lullaby that Grandmother used to sing to me popped into my head and I began to hum it to myself, finding comfort in the melody as I moved in rhythm to the song. I soon calmed down and told myself that it had just been a dream, an amazing one, but just a dream nonetheless. It was then that I heard the foyer clock strike three and I knew I had to move if I was going to get to the theater in time for the audition. I splashed water on my face from the basin on the washstand and it helped considerably. My dress was a wrinkled disaster from sleeping in it, so I quickly changed into the outfit I had so carefully chosen for the audition.

Grandmother was still sleeping. I wondered if the heat was affecting us both—so I took the hack she had arranged for me and made my way over to the theater by myself.

And oftentimes, to win us to our harm
The instruments of darkness tell us truths,
Win us with honest trifles, to betray's
In deepest consequence.

Macbeth Act I, Scene 3

CHAPTER SIX

I have come to understand that there is a certain sacredness in the space of an empty theater. My family would call that blasphemous. However, I have always found that if I sit quietly, either onstage or in the audience of an empty theater it is possible to sense all the emotion that has taken place in that space—the laughter, the tears, the joy, and the fear. I liken it to the feeling an empty church may invoke when one sits quietly and alone in a pew with one's own thoughts. It is a truth, Agnes, that I hope you will come to experience very soon and value.

While what actors do is create a certain artifice, it often evokes real emotion in the audience. It is that emotion that lingers and if you can tune in, it is possible to feel that emotion and know its reality. I believe it is that which makes the space sacred. No other time does this become more apparent than if one is the first to arrive and has a moment or two to become aware of the silence prior to the arrival of the audience or any of the other actors. You can sit in the empty theater and feel it, know it. I happened on this knowledge by accident when I arrived early for my audition with the larger-than-life theatrical impresario, Augustin Daly.

Those few moments I had completely to myself before the audition began were my first experience of tuning into the sacred feeling inherent in an empty theater. As I walked in and onto the stage, I saw that a table and several chairs had been set up on stage left. Stage right had been completely cleared. I stood for a moment on the stage and looked out over the empty audience and felt a kind of reverence. This quickly ended when I heard someone clear their throat directly behind me. I turned to see Teddy Ryan, a concerned expression upon his face.

"Are you all right, Miss Nolan?"

I looked at him in surprise.

"I fell asleep this afternoon and had a dream about Irene Davenport—silly, but it seemed so real," I answered.

I don't know why I said that. A worried look suddenly flashed across his face, but disappeared so quickly, I wasn't sure I had seen it at all.

"Ah, well, it's her role you're trying for, isn't it? And her funeral we had today—perhaps she's been overly in your thoughts," he said, reasonably.

"Perhaps you're right. Of course, that must be it," I said.

It was all I could think to say.

No one else had arrived, so I went over and sat in one of the chairs onstage. I put my purse on the table and took a deep breath to calm my nervousness. Once again, I became aware of how quiet everything was, how empty, and yet, I had a sense of presence about events which had taken place and would take place in this space in the future.

I was roused from these thoughts when Mary appeared, then shortly after, Mr. Daly. He was very kind to both Mary and I, explaining that he wanted a close look at us and thought this arrangement on stage would be so much better than sitting so far away in the audience.

It turned out that there would just be the two of us to audition. After a wait of ten minutes, no other actress in the cast presented herself. This fact succeeded in increasing my nervousness tenfold. Although I was quite sure I wasn't a serious contender, I still had to perform in front of a very critical audience. Besides Mr. Daly, Mr. Hearne and Mr. Portman were present, while Teddy hovered in the background.

I had to remind myself that the real reason I was there was for the hope of making a connection that might further my career in the theater. I felt it was a foregone conclusion that Mary would be given the role of Lady Macbeth.

Mr. Daly asked us to audition one at a time. We could watch each other or not as we chose. Since neither of us had any objection, we both remained seated at the table.

Mr. Daly asked Mary to go first. Her superior experience in the theater quickly became apparent to me. She had put together a costume of sorts to evoke the Scottish flavor of the play. Her hair had been rearranged and I could tell she had stage make-up on. While I had prepared mentally, she had gone the next step. I sensed in her how much she truly wanted this opportunity. She seemed so much more knowledgeable than I and, from the looks of things, much more prepared. My face must have shown my concern.

"I trust you prepared the scene we talked about?" Mr. Daly asked me.

I nodded, unable to speak.

Both Mr. Hearne and Mary walked over to the right side of the stage. They performed the scene where Lady Macbeth encourages, really *demands*, that Macbeth "screw his courage to the sticking place." I have to say it was really well done. Mary showed considerable talent. As nervous as I was, I felt completely taken in by her performance. She did well and I was happy for her.

I could also tell that she knew she had done well. I smiled at her, but when I caught her attention, she didn't seem to respond.

"Well done, Miss Cosgrove," Mr. Daly said.

As she came and sat at the table, I realized my opportunity had arrived and Mr. Daly turned expectantly to me.

Nervous beyond anything I could imagine, at that moment, I also felt a bit hopeless. My mind was racing. How was I going to get through the same scene with as little embarrassment as possible? I couldn't possibly do as well as Mary had done. I rose and walked to the stage right area to take my place next to the waiting Mr. Hearne.

And then, the strangest thing happened. My whole body began to feel light. It is difficult to describe now, but I felt as if I could fly, as if I were about to lift off the stage floor. I felt fluid, insubstantial and the next thing I knew, I was floating above my body, watching my own self stand there.

At the same instant, I became aware of Irene. She stood in front of my body and looked up at me as I floated in mid-air and smiled. It was not a nice smile. She seemed to merge with my body and, in that moment, I no longer had any sensation or memory.

The very next thing I knew, I was back in my body and on my knees on the stage floor. I looked up into the stunned faces of all those around me and felt the dead silence of the room. What had I done? What had just happened? Had I completely embarrassed myself? The first face I became aware of was Mary's and there was a look of such fury and anger upon her countenance, I could not believe that such angelic features could be so contorted. It was gone as quickly as it came and I thought perhaps I had imagined it as part of the state I found myself in.

It was Teddy Ryan who rescued me. He suddenly appeared by my side and gently took me by the arm and helped me to stand. He handed me a glass.

"Drink this," he simply said.

It was water and as warm as it was, it suddenly tasted very good.

Mr. Daly came directly over to me and stood in front of me.

"That was amazing. I believe we have discovered a new theatrical talent. I had no idea that anyone in Eleanor's family possessed such a gift. You did exceptionally well, my dear."

I had no idea *what* he was talking about as I had no memory of what had just taken place. Had I already auditioned? I thought perhaps I had tripped and perhaps that was why I was kneeling on the floor. I looked at the faces around me, but no explanation was forthcoming.

And that was how, after only one night's experience as the Second Gentlewoman with one line, I was given the role of Lady Macbeth and made one of the stars of Mr. Daly's touring company.

One would think that all my desires had suddenly and miraculously been fulfilled. But, I really wanted to know what had happened to me and, to tell the truth, I was deeply frightened. I write these words now some eighty years later, but when I revisit my feelings, the same sense of fear almost overwhelms me. I didn't feel as if I could tell anyone—certainly they would have thought I was utterly and completely mad. I had "seen" Irene Davenport (who, as we all knew, was completely and irrevocably dead) and she possessed my body at the audition. Who could I tell? It was a far stretch, even for Grandmother, to accept. I didn't quite believe it myself, but I had to live with the result. What else was I going to do?

To be honest, I did not even *think* about turning down the role. Well, at first, I felt I should have told Mr. Daly that I couldn't go through with it and that Mary was really the better choice. But then, I realized that this was my chance. This opportunity could launch my career. However, I also knew it would only be until a more suitable and much more famous replacement could be found. My mind raced back and forth, arguing with itself, vanity versus reason versus the yearning to have this incredible opportunity, to perhaps become what I have always wanted.

I have to say, clarity arrived on my Grandmother's doorstep the next morning and once again, it came from an unexpected quarter. James Jr. appeared after another sleepless night that featured no reappearance of Irene Davenport, thank goodness, but no sleep either. I certainly wasn't at my best when he arrived. He bore with him a small bouquet of yellow daisies. Yellow. There was that color again, the one Teddy Ryan had insisted was so unlucky.

That morning, I felt the color was to prove particularly unlucky for James Jr. Grandmother smiled at me as he stood in the front parlor.

"Let me get a vase," she said and left me alone with him, holding, if not the proverbial bag, then a fist full of daisies.

Once alone, James, Jr. launched into his usual monologue.

"I assume you've gotten this out of your system."

"Gotten what out, James?" I asked sweetly.

"The acting, of course. Now that Irene Davenport is dead, the play will close and there will no longer be any need for my future wife to parade herself across a public stage."

"Oh, were you at the opening night?" I asked, knowing he was not.

"Certainly not, I was not going to watch my fiancée show herself off."

"I had no idea we were engaged."

"Of course we are. This is a passing fancy and you will come to your senses."

As tired as I was, exhausted from all that had happened, I had to say my innate curiosity overran any impatience.

"But, why James Jr.? Why do you want to marry me? It seems I am much more trouble than you would ever want. Why?"

I could tell that the question really startled him and I wondered if he had ever really considered it.

"Because I…"

He sat down.

"I really do care for you, Rosemary."

Few things have ever left me speechless. That was one of the first. James Jr. had an emotion for someone other than himself and it was for me. I had never imagined the possibility. I had to sit down myself.

"Oh, James."

It was all I could say.

He looked at me and, during that moment, there was such hope in his face, such longing. Who could not respond to such flat out honesty? I had to be honest with him, as well.

"Oh, James, I really do not want to hurt you, but you must know I do not care for you in the same way."

It didn't seem to upset him.

"I know that, Rosemary. I just want you to think about your future. Now, there's no chance you can go back to the stage. You do understand it's just not respectable and honestly, no other man would be as understanding as I have been. So, you see, this may be—I may be your only chance for a respectable life. I'm willing to forget about this crazy idea of yours—we can even keep it a secret between the two of us—just come to your senses. Be the sensible girl I know you are and forget all this theatrical nonsense."

So much for tender honesty. My response was forthwith and I'm afraid rather brutal.

"It just happens Mr. Augustin Daly does not believe I am nonsensical or without talent. He has just offered me the role of Lady Macbeth—the lead—starring with Mr. Edward Hearne for the foreseeable future. As for a respectable life with you, you can take your flowers and your marriage proposal and no thank you to either one!"

I don't know what stunned him more: the refusal of a respectable life with him or the news of my continuation of a life in the theater. In any case, he suddenly leaped up, strode out of the room, and grabbed his hat off the side table where he had placed it upon his entrance. He turned, as if to say something particularly witty and/or repugnant to me. But, he had difficulty articulating exactly the right thing, so he spun on his heel and exited out the front door, slamming it so hard, the leaded glass shook.

Grandmother appeared from the kitchen where she had evidently been eavesdropping on our conversation.

"I never thought he was the right man for you."

I looked at her and I had to laugh. Then, she laughed and I knew, in the very moment, that I was going to be all right.

At this point, it appeared that all my bridges had been burned. I could not go to Mr. Daly and confess there was no way I could perform the role of Lady Macbeth. Instead, I threw myself into memorizing all my lines and working with Mr. Hearne. The next day was a blur of costume measurements. I was to have my own, as Mrs. O'Neill had packed away all of Irene's things and insisted I get my own make-up. I was given the star dressing room, even though all of Irene's possessions were still there.

Everything had been packed up and moved from her suite at The Sherman House and placed in her dressing room until it could be determined what to do with it all. There, it remained. It was rather eerie having Irene's possessions stacked around the room. Among them was a life size portrait of Irene as Lady Macbeth. I asked Teddy for a dust cover to be placed over it so I didn't have to look at it. He seemed happy to oblige me on that matter.

I sat at the dressing table, contemplating my image in the mirror and wondering for the hundredth time just what I had gotten myself into, when Mary appeared in the mirror behind me. I just about jumped out of my skin.

"Mary! You startled me," I gasped.

"I am so sorry, I didn't mean to. I just came to say–"

"Oh, Mary I–"

"Lillian, it's all right. This time it's you, next time, it might be me."

"I thought your audition was wonderful," I said, helplessly.

"Mr. Daly obviously didn't agree."

"I have to say I wanted it, but hated that you didn't get it, as well."

I wondered who I thought I was. I was acting like James, Jr., for goodness sake! I turned away from the mirror and looked up at her.

She looked down at me.

"It's really all right. In any case, I'm not holding it against you and I really do wish you well."

"Thank you, Mary. That means a lot to me."

She gently touched my shoulder and was gone.

I turned back to the mirror and there was Irene Davenport, standing behind me where Mary had been. I screamed. And promptly fainted.

When I came back to consciousness, I had fallen over backwards and, once again, Teddy Ryan was there, hovering over me. There was a crowd in the doorway.

"There, there. She's all right everyone. No need to panic. Give the girl some room."

I tried to sit up, but Teddy stopped me.

"You've had quite a fright," he said. "Take it easy, let me help you."

He all but lifted me back into my chair. He had somehow managed to obtain a cold compress and was holding it against the back of my neck. It felt absolutely wonderful. Before I let myself relax, however, I noticed that the dressing room was filled with people who had come to see what happened. Mrs. O'Neill, Mary, Mr. Hearne, Miriam, even Mr. Kelly, as well as two girls who were *entr'acte* dancers and one or two of the technicians crowded into the small room.

"The show is over—go about your business," growled Teddy.

They murmured and moved away as I closed my eyes and tried to block the embarrassment from my mind.

"What happened to me?" I asked, quietly.

"I don't know. I heard you scream, so I ran down here and found you on the floor, pale as a ghost. You had a look of pure fright upon your face."

That seemed to me to be an understatement. I tried a joke.

"Teddy, I don't think ghosts are all that pale!"

And then, he said something that startled me very much.

"You've seen her."

Not a question, a statement. All I could do was nod.

"I've known it," he said. "I've sensed it. She was never a nice woman and it doesn't surprise me that she has decided to stay around and haunt the place."

I blurted out how I had seen her before the audition, how my dream had been so real, how she had quoted from Mac—the Scottish Play about "murder."

Teddy paused.

"You must be very careful. It is a vengeful spirit we have here. If you can see her, that means you have the gift. I can only sense her. Sometimes I can feel her, like having the hair rise on the back of your neck. Things can get dangerous for you. Here."

He placed a small silver medal in my hand.

"St. Genesius. The patron saint of actors. Make sure you carry this at all times."

I looked down at the piece of metal in my hand. I was completely unsure as to how this was going to protect me from the continuing appearance of Irene Davenport. I also knew that as kind as Teddy was to me, there was no way I could ever tell him about what happened to me just before the audition. The next night was to be my opening night performance. I had no idea what to do. I couldn't admit that the how and why of me getting the part had nothing to do with the conscious me. On the other hand, I could not accept the other option, which was James Jr. and the unexceptional life that was offered from that direction. Teddy arranged for a cab for me, put me in it and sent me home to Grandmother.

"Rest. That's the thing. You need your strength."

I have to say I didn't disagree with him.

When I arrived home, I discovered Grandmother was having another of her salons. The parlor was filled with her friends and, once more, the center of attention was Cora L. V. Tappan. Grandmother heard me come into the house and met me at the door, a look of concern upon her face.

"My dear, are you all right?"

"I fainted, but I'm all right. I'm just over-tired. How did you know? Did Teddy send a message?"

"Of course not, dear, Cora told me. She said you had a surprise visitor. Who was it?"

"No. No. It was the heat, all the excitement—a bad combination."

Grandmother merely raised one eyebrow at me in that way she does when she wants to express her disbelief.

"I see. Well, come in for a moment."

We walked into the front parlor together.

"Here she is ladies, the new star of Mr. Daly's Chicago production of *Macbeth*! "

Inwardly, I cringed when I heard the name of the Scottish Play, but I shook it off as being silly. I knew all of Grandmother's friends and they surrounded and cooed over me, complimented and congratulated me. It was my very first taste of fame—or at least, notoriety—and I have to say, I enjoyed the attention a great deal. After a discussion that totally centered on me, my thoughts and feelings and what was happening with the play and at the theater, the ladies began to take their leave. One by one, they floated off to other engagements and responsibilities. I felt absolutely wonderful, relaxed and at ease. I had been lulled into a sense of euphoria by all their attention.

Once again, I found myself sitting alone with Mrs. Tappan.

"You have been having some interesting experiences, I think," she said, smiling in that funny way of hers.

That was an understatement.

"You are becoming cognizant of the abilities we spoke of the last time I was here?"

"Is *that* what is happening to me?"

She tilted her head to one side, as if she were listening to a conversation with someone I could not see.

"Yes. And Ouida, my spirit guide, tells me that there is someone there who desperately wants to talk with you. She says she can bring her forth and you can converse, if you want—you have the same ability, but it has not been developed. However, Ouida tells me she is here now."

Before I could respond to her astonishing pronounce-
ment, I noticed that Mrs. Tappan's whole demeanor
changed. She sat more upright in the chair and placed the
glass of lemonade she had been drinking on the side table
next to her. She appeared more regal, more powerful, not
just in the room, but in her presence. It was as if she
suddenly owned the room. I felt a chill go right up my
backbone and I could have sworn that the temperature
dropped in the room by at least ten degrees.

"You think perhaps it was you who obtained the
position, the role in which you find yourself?"

It was Irene Davenport and now, she was *talking* to me.

All I could do was babble.

"I...uh–"

"Ridiculous girl. But, I now find myself in the position
of needing your help and I offer a bargain."

I listened, frozen to my chair as a voice from the land of
the dead outlined what she wanted of me.

"I was murdered. I want to know who and I want you
to find out. I will seek my own revenge. In exchange, you
have an ability that allows me access to your body. You
want fame—I can feel it. I understand it. I can offer you my
talent to work through you. You will experience adulation
and fame, the type of success that an untrained seventeen-
year-old girl—no matter how talented—could ever expect.
But, you must find the person who ended my life. Do you
agree?"

I was mesmerized. The offer in front of me was
unbelievable, fantastic. It solved my problem, released me
from my decision over what to do. Something inside me,
one small, still voice urged me that this was not in my best

interest. I managed to ignore it and my thoughts went to the ladies who were still in the foyer talking to Grandmother. What would it be like to have an entire theater of over a thousand people offering that kind of response and attention to me? What would that be like? I let my imagination run rampant in those very rich and green fields.

Once more, the voice demanded, "Do you consent?"

"Yes. Yes. I will. I will do it."

"Very well," Irene said. "I will help you and you will find my murderer."

Cora's head nodded once and then, Irene was gone. Cora was back. She took a deep breath and smiled at me.

"Did you get the information you needed?"

"Don't you know?"

"Oh, my goodness, no! I am never aware of what takes place when Ouida brings someone through. It would be like taking each and every person's life into my own. Long ago, I learned to protect myself from that personal intrusion. I am just a conduit."

She looked at me, worried now.

"Was it satisfactory?" she asked.

I willed myself to relax.

"Oh, yes. It was unexpected information, but interesting and, in a way, helpful."

"Good. I am glad for you."

It was then that she said something that chilled me to the bone.

"You must be careful with your own abilities, you know. You have mediumistic capabilities. You can be a channel, as well. You must always protect yourself, as it is possible to lose yourself when others—those beyond the veil—may wish to come through. I have Ouida, my Indian guide, who protects me. I sense you have not met your guide yet. You must be exceedingly careful."

The conversation felt like it had taken an inordinate amount of time, but in actuality, it had taken place while Grandmother said farewell to her friends in the foyer and on the front steps. My whole world had shifted and I felt like hours had passed and it had only been minutes.

Grandmother walked back into the parlor.

"Well, I see you've been having a nice chat. Anything interesting?"

Cora spoke up and I panicked, thinking she was about to tell Grandmother about my fantastic agreement. Instead, she said, "I was telling your granddaughter about her own budding abilities. I believe you have an intuitive in your family."

My grandmother looked at me in a new way.

"Oh, really?"

"I believe Mrs. Tappan merely refers to my sense of imagination—you know how developed that has been— and how now, it is serving me so well," I replied.

"Perhaps," Grandmother said. "Let's have some more cake."

And with that, she sat down, picked up her teacup and began a conversation that had nothing whatsoever to do with spiritualism, mediums, or the theater. My thoughts, as she chatted on, were obsessed with all three.

Strange things I have in head that will to hand.
Which must be acted ere they may be scann'd.

Macbeth Act III, Scene 4

~~~~~~

CHAPTER SEVEN

That next night was memorable for a number of reasons. It was, of course, my first opening night in a major role. While Grandmother was there, to my knowledge, not one other member of my family or friends was in attendance. Secondly, James, Jr. did not send flowers, but Grandmother did. Their fragrance permeated my dressing room.

The weather continued to be unremittingly and unseasonably warm for October. I clearly remember things like dressing in my costume and applying my stage make-up. However, I have no memory whatsoever of anything from the first moment I entered the stage for the first scene to the last when I found myself bowing in front an audience that was enthusiastically applauding me. I simply do not know where I went, what I did or how I accomplished the role that night. The house was less than half full, but each member was on his or her feet and the waves of applause felt like so much love and approval to me that I could not help but feed upon it.

After the curtain closed and I walked from the stage, the scenery began to shift. I passed Mr. Hearne and I can only say he appeared slightly stunned.

"Well done, Miss Nolan. Very well done."

The thought raced through my mind—was he the one? Did he kill her? I passed Mary, but she would not look at me. She cast her eyes down and then quickly moved away. As I continued toward my dressing room, Mrs. O'Neill was there. Her entire demeanor had changed. She now seemed pleased to be assigned as my personal dresser.

"Here, let me help you undress, you must be exhausted."

She was so tender, so kind, so totally out of the character I had attributed to her. It occurred to me that people would be treating me differently now; people would be *seeing* me differently. The girl, Rosemary, was disappearing and, in her place, this person, this Lillian Nolan would emerge. But, who was she really? A fraud? Was it really me? Or was it really Irene? I did not dwell on this introspection for very long because it was replaced with an overwhelming urge to begin to look for Irene's killer.

I had no idea how I was going to accomplish this task when Mrs. O'Neill said to me, "You were so like my lady tonight. All you needed was her pearls to complete the image."

The pearls—why hadn't I thought of that? Start with the murder weapon.

"What happened to them, Mrs. O'Neill?"

"Oh, I have them. They are in her trunk." Her eyes took on an excited glow. "Would you like to see them?"

"Yes. Very much."

Mrs. O'Neill took a key from the chain around her waist and unsnapped a single trunk key. She carefully inserted it into the lock and released the catch, opening the trunk. She removed a good-sized lady's leather jewelry box and brought it over. She opened it and it was completely filled with luminescent pearls, all exactly the same size. There were so many of them.

"I gathered up every pearl I could find. I believe I found almost all of them. She was always so proud of them. I don't know what's going to happen to them now."

A tear coursed down her cheek. Here was one person who truly mourned the passing of Irene Davenport, who, in her own way, had loved her. I had not witnessed that depth of emotion from any other person who had been part of Irene's circle of acquaintances. Of course, I was about to expand my own circle of knowledge in that area and who knew what I was going to find?

Mrs. O'Neill moved away to find a handkerchief and dab at the evidence of her emotion. In the meantime, I looked through the pearls, all completely unstrung now and piled into the box, disconnected, except for a small section of the strand. I picked that up and could see instead of string, a thin tensile wire ran through the pearls. The end stuck out of one of the pearls, snapped off as if it had been put through extreme pressure.

"Mrs. O'Neill, did she always wear these?"

"Of course. They were like a signature. Whatever role she played, she wore these pearls. She had, of course, other jewels, but these are the only ones she ever wore on stage."

"How long had she had them?"

"Oh, as long as I have known her—and that's been over twelve years since I came to work for her."

Twelve years. She'd been wearing these for twelve years. That was no secret. Everyone knew she'd wear them opening night—but only one person knew they would become a noose that would kill her.

"Were they always locked up?"

"No. I lock them up now because she's gone and I don't want people putting their hands on her things, but she would often leave them out. She liked looking at them; I think they were part of how she got ready every night, her ritual, I suppose. How she put on the character she would play. After a performance, she would be exhausted and leave them anywhere. After the final dress rehearsal, I couldn't find them. She was furious. I had to tear the room apart until I found them again. She was so worried that someone had taken them. They were right here, though. Safe."

Yes, and re-strung with a wire that had wound around her neck and strangled the life from her, I thought

Mrs. O'Neill took the pearls, lovingly placed them in the case, put that in the trunk and carefully re-locked it. Irene had proven right about one thing: she had been murdered.

There was a knock on the door and Bobby Martin entered, his arms filled with long-stemmed, red roses.

"For you, Miss Nolan."

"Oh, thank you, Teddy. They're lovely. I wonder who they could be from."

A part of me hoped they would be from my parents. I especially wanted some sign, some token from Father. Perhaps he had heard how well the performance went. But, no. They were from Mr. Daly. The card on them read:

My confidence in you has not been misplaced. Well done!

That was my first night in a leading role, my first experience of intuitive abilities and the beginning of my first murder investigation.

The following day, I arrived at the theater early so I could look at the scenery. I wanted to understand exactly how the pearls could have caught on it. Of course, the scenery was not locked away, but out here in the open, accessible to anyone at any time. Anyone could have arranged this. But why? Who wanted to kill Irene?

I began to look at people differently. Suspiciously. I was running the cast over in my mind when I almost walked into the man standing next to Mary backstage. My heart skipped a beat as I looked directly up into the face of the young man that I had seen with Mary at the funeral. He was even taller and much more handsome up close than from a distance. Now, here he was again and only inches away!

"Pardon me, Miss," was all he said, as if it were his fault that I almost rammed into him.

Mary glared at me and I took a step back. However, the good manners that Mother had ingrained into me over the past seventeen years came to my rescue at that moment.

"Mary, I do not believe I have met your friend."

Her enthusiasm for our friendship had completely dimmed and it saddened me because she had been my only friend in the theater. She was the only one who had shown me any kind of true kindness, except for Mr. Hearne, but even his response to me had been more of a polite distraction than anything else.

"Oh, this is an old friend of mine, Jack Martin."

"How do you do, Mr. Martin?"

"Congratulations, Miss Nolan, on your role. I saw your performance last night—you were very good."

His voice was rich and deep. I had to force myself to look away from him so that I did not appear a complete idiot. His compliments were nice, but they were for someone else's ability—one for whom I had no connection. I wanted so desperately to talk to someone about what that was like, but I realized how odd that would sound. I was frustrated because I had no idea what my performances were like; I simply had no memory of them.

I was about to make some inane comment when a voice called out, "Jack!" And Bobby came running up. Mr. Martin began to smile and the polite façade of his face relaxed into one of true emotion.

"Bobby, you staying out of trouble?"

"You know I am, Jack. I see you met Miss Nolan, she's my friend."

It was hard not to like Bobby; he had such enthusiasm and interest for what he was doing.

"Oh, really now?" was all Mr. Martin said.

Bobby turned to me. "He's the brother I told you about. He works for Roger Plant."

"Bobby, that's enough, now," Jack admonished.

Roger Plant was a name I was completely unfamiliar with and Bobby said it like it was someone I should definitely know, someone very important. Mary and Jack exchanged a quick look.

"And I'd best be getting back to work, as well," Jack said.

Mary had been silent during the exchange, but now she said that was probably wise. Jack sighed, tipped his hat to the both of us and took his leave. Bobby walked with him to the stage door entrance and I turned to watch him leave.

"He's a handsome man, isn't he Lillian?"

That broke my reverie and I flushed and immediately turned back to her.

"Is he? I really hadn't noticed."

Mary laughed. "Then, you're not that great an actress, after all."

I blushed and, with that, she walked away.

I couldn't tell how she felt for Jack—if she felt the same for him as my relationship with James Jr., or if it was something much more. Or, perhaps she was just still mad at me. I desperately wanted to make peace with her. I so wanted a friend. I walked after her.

"Mary, please, can't we just be friends? I didn't really expect...your friend seems very nice," I finished, lamely.

She turned back and looked at me.

"Lillian, Jack and I have known each other a very long time and we are close friends, but that's all."

She paused then and said, "You must know this is all very hard for me. I really deserved that role. I wanted it and I worked so hard and you just walked off with it. Everything is so easy for you—you have no idea how hard things have been for me and I thought I was finally going to get a break. I'm sorry, it's just going to take me a while."

She turned and walked down the stairs to the dressing rooms. A thought flitted across my mind that if she was nice enough to me before opening night, why the change now? It came to me that she must have thought I was going to fall flat on my face and, when I didn't, she became angry. She was jealous of me, of my talent. And then, I took a deep breath because I realized I did not know where that thought came from. It was so unlike me.

I was interrupted from my musings when Bobby came over to me.

"Jack really loves her, I think, but she won't give him the time of day. She wants to be a big actress–"

"Yes, I suppose she does."

I now knew I had to stay away from Jack Martin. Mary would never be my friend if I took the role she wanted and the man she cared for. I suddenly felt rather guilty, remorseful for having stolen something someone else had wanted so desperately, especially since it wasn't really me who earned it. I wasn't feeling very charitable towards myself at that moment. And once again, Bobby broke into my thoughts.

"Oh, my brother got me a job here and it's a good one. I'm hoping to keep it and work my way up."

Thank God for Bobby. I turned to him and asked, "Up to what?"

"I want to be a stage manager like Teddy—Mr. Ryan."

"Well, you do a very fine job indeed, Bobby, and I would not be surprised at all if in a few years, you weren't a stage manager."

He puffed himself up at that as only a thirteen-year-old can and once again, I was reminded of my own little brother, Francis, and how he reacted that way when he was complimented—only for him, it was usually after a particularly good sports achievement. I thought about the disparity between the two of them. Francis wouldn't have to think about earning a living until he had graduated from some college and then, I was sure Father would want him in business with him. I suddenly felt a great loss over the pain I was causing in my family and it must have shown on my face.

"Is something wrong, Miss Nolan?"

"No, no, I was just thinking about my brother–"

"You have a brother?"

"Two of them."

"What are they like?"

"Well, they play sports, mostly."

"Do they come to the theater?"

"I think they would like to, but it's difficult right now…"

"Can they read?"

"Of course they can."

"I wish I could."

I thought about my family and wondered if there was something I should do to try and contact them. No one except Grandmother had come to the theater and very soon, Mr. Daly would announce that he had found an actress to take over the tour. I couldn't do anything about them, but I could do something for the boy standing in front of me.

"I could teach you."

"What?"

"Teach you to read."

"You'd do that?"

"Sure. We'll start tomorrow, all right?"

He smiled and his entire face lit up. I heard Teddy call for him.

"Bobby, I need you to run an errand."

"Got to go. See you, Miss Nolan. And thanks."

"Goodbye, Bobby."

Just then, Teddy came up behind me and said, "Anything I can do for you, Miss Nolan?"

Startled, I almost jumped straight up.

"Sorry, didn't mean to scare you," he said.

"Oh, it's all right."

"Did you hear someone whistling in the theater last night?

"No, I didn't," I answered.

"Not a good thing, you know. Means the play will end soon. Summons the devil, it does. Terrible bad luck to whistle in a theater. Don't know what they were thinking. If I find out who, I'll certainly give them a piece of my mind."

"I didn't know that."

"I would say there are a lot of things you don't know about working in a theater, Miss Nolan."

"That's very true, but I've also learned a great deal."

"Yes. And are you sure you know what it is you're doing?"

I could not respond. I could not imagine he knew about my bargain with Irene, so I could only assume he meant to reference my inexperience on stage. I straightened my shoulders and said with my best authoritative voice, "I know exactly what I'm doing, Mr. Ryan."

He nodded at that and walked away. I realized I wasn't making any friends among the people I so desired to work with. Nothing was the way I wanted it to be. I was nowhere near close to the answer to the question of who wanted Irene dead. I called after him.

"Teddy, I'm sorry. I have just been under such pressure. I didn't mean to be rude."

He visibly relaxed.

"Alright, Miss."

"Can I ask you a question? About Irene Davenport?"

"Ah, what about her?"

"Well, what was she like?"

"I think you know she was very talented, very popular. A famous actress."

"Yes, but you worked with her. What was she like, as a person?"

Before Teddy could form an answer, the question was answered for him.

"Well, that's a hard question, but I have to say, with all honesty, that she was a truly awful woman. I, for one, am relieved that I no longer have to perform onstage with her."

I hadn't heard Mr. Hearne come in, but now as he stood in the semi-darkness of the theater, it was obvious that he had heard our conversation. Teddy sighed.

"But, that would be speaking ill of the dead, right, Mr. Hearne?"

"Oh, Theodore, I told her exactly the same thing to her face, so that certainly doesn't apply. The truth is, Miss Nolan, Irene Davenport would have cut her own mother out of a role if she wanted it. Never felt anyone else had as much ability as she herself did. She didn't value anyone else's talent, only her own. She was difficult and she was demanding. While, you, my dear," and he took my hand, lifted it up to his face and brushed a kiss against it, "are so very much nicer to deal with."

I must have blushed to the roots of my scalp because he laughed and dropped my hand before turning and going on his way. If charm had a name, it would certainly be Edward Hearne. He bowed and continued on down the stairs to the dressing rooms, swinging the ebony cane he always carried.

Teddy brought me back into awareness. "Well, there was certainly no love lost between the two of them. They couldn't stand each other. The animosity went back years."

"But, they were in the same play."

"You'll find that happens more often than not—two actors who are cast as the love interest to one another have to make the audience believe they are mad *for* each other onstage and all they really are is mad *at* each other offstage. They barely tolerated each other. I believe Mrs. Davenport downright hated him."

I marveled at this.

"But why? He's so handsome and so charming."

"I think it may have had something to do with the fact that, at one time, she was interested in him, but he would have none of her—or any woman—if you get my drift."

I had no idea what Teddy was talking about. How could any man not be attracted to a beauty like Irene Davenport? Of course, I was very young and I'm so much older and more experienced now. The theater attracts talented and driven people from all sorts of life experiences and proclivities. I think that it also allows for a certain sense and sensitivity that is not permitted in most other lines of work. Over the years, I have met and known so very many people and had the opportunity to observe them at their most vulnerable times. For an actor is most vulnerable when he or she puts himself or herself out there for display, looking for approbation and never knowing if one will receive it or be condemned or criticized for it. It is a very punishing and exhilarating line of work.

I did have a sense that Edward Hearne was a keenly sensitive man and his heart had been pierced by Irene's intensive dislike and disapproval of him. What had she done to him and how far would he go to seek his revenge? Far enough to consider murder?

That night, as I was getting ready for the performance, I thought about the diverse personalities that made up the actors who performed in this play. I suddenly became aware that Mrs. O'Neill was looking for something. More like tearing the room apart.

"What are you looking for, Mrs. O'Neill?"

"The brooch, the brooch. Have you seen it? Did you take it?"

I had no idea what she was talking about. Since I was already closer to Irene Davenport than I was comfortable with, which was most assuredly quite enough for me, I never felt the need to go through any of her things in order to evoke her presence.

"No. I haven't touched anything. Besides, the trunk is locked."

"It's gone and I can't find it."

"What's gone?"

She looked at me as if I was an idiot child.

"The Celtic brooch that Mrs. Davenport always wore on her costume. I saw it yesterday, but today it's gone."

"Perhaps you just misplaced it, put it somewhere else."

Mrs. O'Neill stopped, straightened her shoulders.

"I was Mrs. Davenport's dresser and assistant for twelve years. I never misplaced anything. It's gone, I tell you. Someone has stolen it."

She looked right at me as she said this.

"I believe I will have a few words with Mr. Ryan. There is a thief in the theater."

And with that, she strode out of the dressing room, a woman on a righteous mission.

I had no idea what could have happened to the brooch and my first reflection on the matter was that Irene had been buried with it. But, according to Mrs. O'Neill, that was incorrect. I also thought it strange that of all of Irene's possessions, that one particular article would be taken—a round, Celtic brooch with a large pin through it. The pin kept her tartan shawl in place and I remembered seeing her wear it on her costume on opening night. It was also included in the painting of her as Lady Macbeth.

I stood now and walked over to the life-sized painting, which leaned against the back wall of the dressing room and was covered by a dust cloth. I removed the cover and looked at the painting. There stood Irene, absolutely resplendent in her costume, the pin clearly shown on her right shoulder. While the artist managed to capture her beauty, there was a certain hardness depicted in the line of her jaw that revealed a woman in possession of a rare, fierce determination. I wondered who that woman truly was. What brought her here and who had taken her life?

The temperature dropped suddenly in the room and I could feel her presence. A chill went up my neck and down my spine. There was a whisper—the faintest voice—which I knew did not come from my own thought and it invaded my mind.

"Murder most foul."

The line from *Macbeth*. Irene was reminding me of my purpose. It was a task that I felt less and less enthusiasm for. I took a deep breath and expelled it all at once. The room had grown so cold that I could see my breath, but, as suddenly as it came, it was gone.

It will have blood, they say; blood will have blood…

Macbeth Act III, Scene 4

~~~~~~

CHAPTER EIGHT

That very next afternoon, I walked into my dressing room and was amazed to see Mother sitting stiffly upright on the edge of the chaise lounge. She looked uncomfortable—as if she was afraid she would get her dress dirty if she leaned back. Mrs. O'Neill was busy puttering around and, by the silence between them, I could tell neither one was thrilled with the presence of the other. Mrs. O'Neill saw me first, gave me a haughty look and walked out.

"Hello, Mother."

"Oh, Rosemary!"

She jumped up, ran over to me and embraced me. I was overwhelmed with emotion and immediately returned her embrace. No matter what, Mother loved me and I loved her. I reveled in how good it felt just to see her and be with her. It was as if, for that moment, there had been no disagreement, no estrangement between us.

"Your father wants you to come home."

"Does he?"

"He loves you Rosemary."

"And you, Mother, how do you feel?"

She paused for a moment.

"I've gone over those hateful words I said the last time we spoke and I came to say I'm sorry."

This threw me into complete disarray. Mother was apologizing to me?

"Oh, Mother, I am sorry too."

There was a pause, neither one of us seemed to know what to do or say next, so I changed the subject.

"How are John William and Francis?"

"They miss you, too."

"I wish I could see them. "

"You can, you know. All you have to do is come home. Give up your ideas about—," she gestured with her right hand, indicating the whole room, "this place."

"And marry James Jr."

"Well," Mother smiled, "I think your father would even let you forego James Jr. if you did the former two."

We both smiled at that. It was so good to be with her. Grandmother was wonderful and I loved her dearly, but she was cake and icing. My family was the bread and butter of my life.

"I can't, Mother. I've dreamed of this my whole life."

"Is your dream so important that you are willing to give up your family for it? Your father remains adamant."

"I know," I sighed.

"What is the attraction?"

"Why must I choose between you?"

She looked away from me and around the dressing room and, for the first time, I saw it though her eyes. There was no magic here for her. It was a completely ordinary, dusty, cluttered room. Bits of this and that were scattered around the semi-ugly room, the make-up table was messy, and while Mrs. O'Neill kept it fairly clean, it was cluttered and ordinary. I loved it, but I knew it was impossible for Mother to share my enthusiasm.

Mother picked up a sash from across the back of the chaise. She had no way of knowing that was a costume piece set there for a particular reason—a change later in the play. It was specifically placed for convenience and speed. She began to fold it. I knew she was very nervous then. Mother never did household chores if she could help it, preferring to leave them to Jane, who really managed our home. She smoothed it out, making every corner match perfectly, taking her time.

Finally she said, "I don't want to argue with you, Rosemary."

"Mother, why did you come?"

"I wanted to see you, of course."

"Did Father send you?"

She looked up at that.

"No. No. He doesn't even know I'm here. If he knew I was here…well, he would be displeased."

From her reaction, one would think Father was some kind of ogre. In reality, he worshiped Mother and, while he might frown over her decision to come and see me, I just couldn't imagine him even going to the point of displeasure with her.

"It's me."

And then, she burst into tears.

"I want you to come home. I so miss you."

I was shocked. My heart opened and I burst into tears. She reached for me and we clung together. I was about four inches taller than she and all I could think was what a sight we made—clutching each other and crying our eyes out. I had never seen Mother cry before. And, here I was, the one who had brought her to tears! One would have thought there had been a death in the family.

Gus, our theater cat, padded in and jumped up on the dressing table. Gus and I had become fast friends since my first day and I had learned to love him, even though he was an exceptionally independent cat and did not appear to have favorites. He regarded us very seriously and that is what broke my mood.

I laughed out loud. Startled, my mother pulled away.

"You think this is funny?"

"No, it's Gus."

"Gus?"

Gus had begun to clean himself, but he stopped at the mention of his name and fixed his golden eyes upon her.

"You have a cat."

The emotion of the moment seemed to have evaporated, leaving us both a little drained and off balance.

"Gus doesn't belong to anyone. It is good luck to have a cat in the theater."

My mother went over to him and began to scratch him behind his ears, just the way he liked it. He purred his deep purr of absolute content.

"He's lovely."

"Yes, but not completely domesticated."

"No cat ever is, dear."

She gave him a final pat and turned back to me.

"Will you come home, Rosemary?"

I looked at Gus and he contemplated me, as well, as if to ask "Well? What are you going to do?" He must have gotten an answer because he jumped down from the dressing table to the chaise lounge and curled up in the middle of it.

"Mother, I have a commitment here."

"You have a commitment to your family."

"What about the commitment to me and to myself? I have to do this. I want to do this. I have to know—"

"You have to know what?"

She was angry now and I could hear it in the tone of her voice.

"I have to know if I can have something of my own. Something I can do. Something that comes from me and nobody else. Something…a life that is entirely my own."

"I see."

But, I could tell she didn't see at all. Her life was wrapped up in the lives of her husband and her children. I saw in that instant that she lived and breathed for us, so she could never understand a life of her own.

I could feel her pull away.

"So, this is your decision?"

"Yes, Mother."

Her need to support her children was great, but her need to agree with her husband was greater. At that moment, I felt so sorry for her. A part of her was being ripped out and I could do nothing to assuage her pain. I had to pursue my life.

"Very well."

She straightened her hat. She removed her gloves from her purse and put them on. She did not look at me. But suddenly, she grabbed my chin and looked me straight in the eye.

"Rosemary, the door is open for you to come home. I cannot guarantee how long it will remain open. Your father is very angry with you and that door will not remain open forever. I urge you to consider the repercussions of what you are doing."

She dropped her hand and walked out the door.

I collapsed onto my chair in front of the dressing table and the next thing I knew, Gus was in my lap. He stretched his front paw out, reached up and touched my shoulder and then, he rubbed his face against my chin. I utterly refused to cry, but tears streamed down my face, regardless. I stroked Gus and we remained that way for some time until I heard Bobby knock on the door.

"Miss Nolan!"

Gus jumped down and I grabbed a handkerchief to wipe my face.

"Come in, Bobby."

He walked in full of youthful enthusiasm. There was a slate in his hand and box of chalk. I remembered my promise to teach him to read. I could do something right.

"I was wondering if this is a good time–"

"Of course. This is a perfect time. I'm so glad you found a slate." It would get my mind off my family and give me a purpose.

"Jack got it for me."

I pulled up another chair close to mine.

"He wants you to learn to read?"

"He says it's important if I'm going to go anywhere in the world."

"He is so right. How fortunate you are to have such a brother."

"That I am, Miss," he said, solemnly.

"Sit right here and we'll get started," I said, patting the chair and he came and sat down next to me.

And so, we spent a pleasant hour together before I had to get ready for the performance and he had to return to his duties. Bobby was a quick study and he wrote and re-wrote his ABC's several times before we had to stop for the day. We agreed that he would come in at the same time tomorrow and we would continue where we left off. Bobby went off to perform his regular pre-performance duties and I turned to the woman in the mirror and began to apply my make-up.

That night, I performed and, once again, I had no memory of anything that happened. I took no joy in the fact that the audience was now filled to capacity. The newspapers referred to me as the "Unknown Phenomenon" and people showed up in droves to see this new curiosity. I received another telegram from Mr. Daly expressing his thanks for the wonderful effect I was having on the Chicago audiences. I felt rather hollow about it all. What was the point? It really wasn't me on stage. Did I even have any real talent? People were not connecting with me, but rather the shadow of a woman who was gone.

I sat in "our" dressing room that night well after the play had ended. Mrs. O'Neill had left in a huff some time ago. I knew she still suspected me of taking the missing pin. I had tried my best to assure her that I would never touch anything of Irene's without her express approval, but I could tell she did not believe me. It would be some time before I felt she would trust me again. So I lingered. I changed out of my costume and now was slowly removing the last bits of my makeup. It was very late and I knew I should go home to Grandmother's and go to bed, but I wanted to be by myself for a little while longer. The memory of Mother's visit continued to plague me.

I sighed and gathered my things, putting as much order to my dressing table as I could, but leaving the make-up box a mess. It was against my nature, but Teddy had warned me that it was terrible bad luck for an actor to have an orderly make-up kit during the run of a show. I briefly wondered what was more terrible than Irene's death.

I walked out of my dressing room, down the hall, and up the stairs, past Teddy's desk. He saw me and nodded when I said good night. At this point, it was well past one in the morning.

In the alley, the air was still unseasonably warm for early October and I couldn't catch a fresh breath. Everything was very still, very quiet, and very hot. As I walked down the alley, I saw a bundle of what appeared to be discarded clothes and then, I noticed a foot sticking out one end with a well-worn, brown shoe on it.

I approached cautiously and saw that it was Bobby Martin, lying at a strange angle. At first, I thought what an odd place for him to choose to take a nap. Then, I knew he wasn't sleeping, for jammed straight into the middle of his chest was the pin from Irene Davenport's Celtic brooch. I screamed for Teddy and heard the stage door bang open just before I slid down and into unconsciousness.

When I awoke, I was laying on the small cot in Teddy's office. There was a compress on my head. Teddy sat on a stool next to the cot, a worried expression on his face.

"Oh Teddy, poor Bobby!" I clutched at him and he put his arm around me.

"Indeed, it was," Teddy said. "I've sent for your Grandmother. She should be here soon. This is terrible, terrible. Jack is here and wonders if he could have a word with you—and the police are on their way here, as well."

I nodded and sat up. "I'm alright, really I am. It was just such a shock," I said.

I didn't have any time to prepare myself before Jack walked in. It hadn't occurred to me to ask how Jack had gotten to the theater so quickly. But, here he was.

"Miss Nolan."

"Oh, Mr. Martin, I'm so sorry about Bobby."

Tears began to stream down my face without warning.

"Did you see anybody—hear anything?"

"No, no I just was leaving for the night and I walked out and there he was. I'm so sorry."

He sat down on Teddy's stool. I sat across from him on the cot.

"He was all I had."

"Bobby told me just this afternoon what a great brother you are."

"It was my job to look out for him. I didn't do such a good job making sure he was safe. I got him out of the Underworld only to have this happen to him!"

"I don't understand—the Underworld?"

He looked at me with some pity.

"Of course you don't. I imagine there are places in Chicago you have no idea exist. Not too far from here is a place called Conley's Patch. It's a regular den of the worst sort the city has to offer. Bobby and I grew up there. If you have talent or drive or both, you get out. I worked my way up and then I got him out. I thought he would be safe here." He stood up.

"Oh, Miss, what am I going to do without him?"

I got up and patted him on the shoulder, but he burst into tears. He seemed so terribly young then and so vulnerable. I realized he really wasn't all that much older than John William, so I just put my arms around him and tried to make soothing noises, but I had no idea what to say.

At that particular moment, Mary walked into the office. She took in the scene and her face hardened. Jack looked up and saw her there. He immediately left me standing and went to her, throwing his arms around her.

"He's gone, Mary, he's gone."

Her face softened and arranged into its normal angelic lines, her arms cradled him and she began to rock him.

"Oh, Jack. It will be alright. It will be alright."

I moved by them as quickly and as silently as I could, carefully shutting the door behind me. Jack's pain was a terrible thing to behold and his sobs were difficult to hear.

Outside, the alleyway was blocked by police. Teddy was there and he introduced me to the officer in charge, a young man who didn't seem overly concerned about what had happened to Bobby. Our conversation was short and, when we were done, Teddy suggested he walk me through the empty theater and out the front doors.

The sky was just beginning to lighten when he helped me into the hired cab. Grandmother was sitting in it, waiting for me and she held out her arms and I fell into them. My emotions poured out in the comfort of that loving embrace. I sobbed for Bobby and for myself and my family until I could not cry any longer. When we arrived at her house, she helped me out of the cab, up the steps and into the house. She got me up to my room and into bed.

Almost immediately, I fell into a deep sleep. The world and everything else was shut out in the dark abyss of nothingness.

The next day, I woke up and had no idea what time it was. The curtains were drawn and I was terribly hot. All my clothes were wet with sweat and the discomfort of their dampness woke me up. With great effort, I pulled myself upright and sat for a moment on the edge of the bed. My whole body felt heavy; my clothes weighed me down and it was as if I was walking through a world of water. Every movement took great effort. I was completely disoriented and didn't even know where I was. I stood up and almost sat right back down. It was as if every muscle in my body had lost its strength. Leaning on the bed, the chair and finally, the dresser, I made my way to the washstand. Cupping the warm water in my hands, I splashed it against my face and then, my neck and chest. My clothes were now soaked, but I didn't care—I felt as if the water brought me back to life and with that life came the memory of the events of the night before. The pain of Bobby's death hit me all over again.

I had never known anyone who I cared about who died and now I had intimately experienced two deaths. Grandfather had passed when I was very young and I had no memory of him. Irene's death was dreadful, but I had neither known, nor cared for her. Bobby's death was personal and it was awful. It made me feel, once more, the separation from my family. Bobby had been Francis' age and I couldn't even imagine how painful it would have been if it was my little brother's body I had found. I took a deep breath and another one, got out of my wet clothes, put on a clean nightgown and a wrapper and began to feel better. At least I was dry.

There was a tap on the door and Grandmother peeked in.

"Thank God you're finally awake! I was considering calling the doctor."

"What time is it?"

"Three o'clock in the afternoon."

I had slept over ten hours! It didn't seem possible.

"I'll have Cook prepare something to eat. You must be famished."

At first, I didn't think I could ever eat again and then, my stomach let out such a growl that I knew I had better satisfy it.

"Alright."

"Why don't you come down to the front parlor and I'll have it ready for you. It's a little cooler there."

I nodded and she left. Moving very slowly, I was able to navigate the hallways and the stairs. My body ached. By the time I reached the parlor, the food had arrived—toast and currant jelly, scrambled eggs, coffee. It smelled wonderful and Grandmother sat quietly as I slowly ate the food, savoring every bite. Eventually, I felt as if I would revive. Finally, I could eat no more.

"You look better. I was so worried when you didn't wake up."

"Grandmother, it was awful. Bobby was the same age as Francis. He was a dear and so excited about working in the theater. Who could have done such a thing?"

"Who do you think?"

"I don't know. I just don't know."

If I tried to tell her about how Irene had taken possession of me, she would have thought me mad, although a part of me knew nothing I said would ever change her feelings about me. Instead, I told her how the pearls had been restrung with wire and how I was sure that something had happened to Irene, that it hadn't been an accident. I told her that the night before the performance, Mrs. O'Neill had been looking for the brooch and the pin and it was that same pin that had been used to kill Bobby. I knew they were connected.

Her response surprised me.

"Well, of course, dear, Bobby must have seen something or maybe even the person who killed Irene. Or someone must have thought he did."

In the middle of this discussion, the doorbell rang and I heard Father's voice out in the foyer. My heart leaped with hope that he had come because he was truly concerned about me! He walked directly into the parlor, not waiting for the maid to announce him. Grandmother stood to greet him.

"Ah, Walter, it's so nice of you to come and visit me," she said.

He gave Grandmother a quick kiss on her cheek. Then he opened his arms and I flew into them.

"Father," I cried.

He wrapped me in a fierce embrace, almost crushing me.

"Oh, Rosemary, what are we going to do about you?" he said to me.

It was the last thing I wanted to hear at that moment. I pulled back and amazed myself when I merely said, "What do you mean?" I looked into his eyes and they were filled with an emotion I had never seen before.

"Don't tell me that with all that's happened you still haven't gotten this insane plan to be an actress out of your system? I want you to come home and marry as you ought."

The concept of marriage to James Jr. reared its ugly head once again.

I let the question about my being an actress pass and addressed the real issue.

"He's all wrong for me, Father; we really don't suit one another."

"I have no idea what you mean. If you married him, your future would be assured."

Once again, I looked down the long, dull road of life with James Jr. and was convinced my life would most assuredly be fixed and predictable.

"I'm not going to marry James Jr. We've been through this."

He turned to Grandmother.

"This is your influence!"

"Now, calm down, Walter, I know you're not really here to talk about James Jr."

"No. Well, yes, but–"

He took a rather deep breath and let it out.

"Rosemary, I just found out there was *another* death at that theater last night. I've been so worried about you and now this. What if it had been you?"

"Oh, Father." He really was concerned about me.

For a moment my eyes held his and then he looked away.

"You know how concerned your mother and I have been about this whole business. We want you to stop and come home now. I will contact Mr. Daly."

"Father. I can't. I made a commitment. I gave my word. I have to see it through."

"To theater people! As if they counted!"

It flashed through my mind the kindness and consideration I had received from those people. Teddy, who was my guardian angel. Mr. Hearne, polite and patient with me. Even Mrs. O'Neill had been helpful. Mary had been kind at first and I still hoped we could be friends. And then, of course, Bobby Martin.

"Father, please don't worry. In less than a week, Mr. Daly will have found a new actress for the role and my work will be done. It's such a short time and it means everything to me. Can't you understand? Haven't you ever wanted anything so badly, you would do almost anything to achieve it?"

I looked in his hazel eyes—so like my own, indeed, exactly like mine—and saw an expression on his face I had never seen before. It was as if he was remembering something important that was long forgotten. And then, it was gone. He turned to Grandmother.

"Mother, do you have anything to say?"

"Dear Walter. She's right, you know. You, better than anyone I know, understand commitment. You two are so like one another. You have to let her do this. She may get it out of her system, as you say, or it may be so completely ingrained in her that to sever it from her may cause irreparable damage. Is that a risk you are willing to take?"

"I want her to come home. I want her to settle down and do what's right. I want her to be safe."

Then she said, "Because that is what you did?"

I had no idea what she meant by that remark, but before I could ask, he stood up. "Come home now and give up your insane idea about becoming an actress or so help me—"

The moment of connection between us had passed. He had chosen to go back to the role of authoritarian and I responded to him the only way I could.

"I will never marry James Jr. I am an actress and you and Mother will just have to accustom yourselves to it!"

There ensued yet another argument of major proportions. I don't know why I stood up to him so vehemently. I had never done so before; I had always been a dutiful daughter, obedient to both my parents. I truly didn't know if it was because I wanted to be in the theater, which I did, or because I would have none of James Jr. Or it may well have been the influence of Irene Davenport. In any case, it forced Father into an ultimatum.

"What is it going to be, Rosemary? The theater or your family? You can't have both!"

He was asking me to cut myself in two. He believed I couldn't have both and he forced me to choose. The pain was almost unbearable, but so filled with anger was I at that point that I didn't even think when I said, "You'll all have to learn to live without me then."

That either stunned or hurt him so deeply that he could not reply. I could tell he hadn't thought it a possibility that I would respond in such a way. But, it was out now and I couldn't call it back. At that precise moment, I didn't want to. There was a silence then, thick and palpable.

"You mother and I will never forgive you for this Rosemary," Father said, very quietly.

And he walked out of the room and out of the house. I felt with all my heart at that moment that I would never see him again.

Grandmother jumped up and ran after him.

"Walter, Walter–"

She caught up to him on the front porch, but their discussion was short. I was still shaking with anger when Grandmother came back.

"He is quite adamant, my dear. Are you so very sure you want this so much?"

I sat down and once again, my emotions got the best of me, surprising myself in the process—I thought I had none left after the night before. What was happening to me?

It wasn't much later that I had to be at the theater. Just before I went onstage and Irene took over, I swore I heard her cruel and sarcastic laughter, then the words, *you are just like me.*

I didn't want to be like Irene Davenport. From what I had discovered, no one had any love for her. And I didn't particularly care for her, either. I was beginning to feel a blurring of the lines between us. I began to wonder where she left off and where I began. Every day, I felt as if I was losing a little of myself and taking on more of her. I worried that she would take over and I would completely lose myself. And that was very frightening, indeed.

Unnatural deeds
Do breed unnatural troubles; infected minds
To their deaf pillows will discharge their secrets;
More needs she the divine than the physician.

Macbeth Act V, Scene 1

CHAPTER NINE

Mrs. O'Neill was nowhere in sight when I entered my dressing room just two hours later. I noticed Irene's large trunk was unlocked. It was an invitation I could not ignore. I closed the dressing room door and bolted it. I had just enough time before my "appearance" in the first act to go through the trunk and I wanted to know much more about Irene.

Her make-up box was in there, each item in loving order. I quickly discarded that. I took out the costumes for *Macbeth*. She had one for each scene in which she appeared, all designed especially for her. The cut and fabrics were all quite beautiful. I couldn't help but admire them. I found it very difficult not to hold each one up in front of me and look in the mirror. Reluctantly, I set those down. There was the case with the pearls and various other pieces of jewelry.

I put that aside as well, and then I came to the bottom of the trunk. I thought that must be all, everything she brought with her for the play. I decided to look through some of her other belongings. There were other trunks with her "street" clothes, which had been brought over from The Sherman House after her death. Nothing of any interest.

I repacked her costume and shut the lid of the trunk sharply in frustration. I heard a thump. Curious, I opened the heavy trunk lid wide and let it drop on its own. There it was again—the same thump—as if something substantial had shifted. I quickly examined the inside lid of the trunk, running my fingers lightly over the lining and that is when I found a catch, cleverly woven into the pattern of the fabric. I pulled at it and a small door opened. An expensive leather bound book fell into my hand. I opened it and saw it was filled with small, tight, close handwriting. I had found Irene's personal diary.

The temperature in the room began to drop and I had the distinct feeling that Irene was not pleased. Just then, there was a sharp rap on the door and I dropped the diary into the trunk.

Teddy's voice called, "Ten minutes, Miss Nolan."

I took a deep breath.

"Thank you, Teddy."

I began to repack the other trunks, making sure that the contents were just as I had found them. I knew Mrs. O'Neill would be aware if anything had shifted, but I doubted she knew about the diary. I made sure the lid of each trunk was back in place. Convinced that all was in order, I put the diary in my purse, unlocked the door, sat down and finished putting on my make-up. I was inordinately pleased with my find; I was convinced I would come to know the real Irene Davenport and confident that the mystery of her death would be solved.

That night, Irene punished me. She did not appear. As I stood backstage, the normal feeling of lightness did not come over me and I realized I was on my own. Once again, I heard the faint echo of her cruel laugh and I knew this was her retribution for finding the diary. I had to go onstage by myself.

Of course, I knew the lines. I knew I could walk through it, but the house had been full for the last few days of people who wanted to see the prodigy—the girl who slipped into Irene's shoes, as it were. The new talent. At that moment, I realized I was alone. I stepped onto the stage and found myself in the light, dimly aware of the rustle of over 2,000 members of the audience there to see me.

Looking back, I know I did the very best job I was capable of at that time. Probably it was better than most, but I certainly wasn't the caliber of Irene Davenport. By the Third Act the attendance had dropped off considerably. I became aware of the presence of the other actors, standing in the wings while I was onstage. After one exit, Mr. Hearne said to me, "Are you quite well, Miss Nolan?" I had missed a cue and he had covered for me, had saved me. I just nodded, not trusting myself to speak. What was really rather disturbing was the presence of Mary Cosgrove. She stood in the wings, watching every moment, as if she was waiting for something. Had she always been there and I was just completely unaware? She had an odd expression on her face—one of strange satisfaction.

After my last exit, she came up to me.

"Don't worry, Lillian, you had an off night, it happens. You'll be fine." She said this with such kindness, such compassion in her voice. It was hard to see her eyes in the dim light and I welcomed her understanding and hoped we could be friends again.

After I returned home to Grandmother's, I remembered I had Irene's diary. I went up to my room, and removed the slim volume from my handbag. I opened it up and began to read.

For the most part, Edward Hearne was correct. Irene Davenport had been a truly awful woman. There must have been other volumes though, because this diary made numerous references to previously recorded events. These were either hidden somewhere else or she had destroyed the previous volumes when they were full. Somehow, I felt that was correct. There was a tremendous amount of vitriol aimed at other actors, promoters, generally, anyone who was perceived as being in her way on any level. The diary began as she traveled to Chicago from New York. She wrote each day, religiously, but sometimes no more than a line or two about some injury or slight that had occurred. Even her reference to Mr. Samuel Connelly was one of disdain. She had indeed planned on leaving the theater and using him as the vehicle for her "retirement," but she had no use for him, only his money. Suddenly, I felt that Mr. Connelly had escaped a future much worse than mine would have been with James Jr.

I thought how difficult it must have been to live your life like that and why? Why was there so much hatred for everyone and everything? The diary offered no explanation.

It was getting late, and although I wanted to finish the diary, I could no longer keep my eyes open and Irene's small and meticulous writing began to blur, the words running together. I turned off the gas, lay back on my bed and almost immediately fell into unconsciousness.

Once again, Irene appeared in my dreams. We were in a forest and it was well known to me. I walked down a familiar pathway and came upon Irene who was in a complete panic. She was lost and could not find her way out. I tried to tell her I knew the way, but she would not listen. She paced back and forth and then, she would run down one path, only to return a moment later, even more agitated. She wouldn't listen to me and was becoming more and more terrified. Then, she looked past my shoulder and said, "You did this to me."

I turned around to see who she meant, but there was no one there. A strange light was glowing in the distance and I heard the crackle of burning wood. The forest was on fire! I looked around, but there was no escape; the fire had completely surrounded us. Bobby Martin suddenly appeared. He looked relaxed and happy and seemed at ease.

"This way, Miss," he said.

I knew I had to follow him. The smell of smoke grew stronger and I started to cough. It became harder and harder to follow Bobby, to even see him in the haze of smoke and fire. Coughing racked my body and it was that coughing that finally woke me up. I continued to cough and my lungs eventually cleared until I was able to breathe again. There was a lingering scent of smoke in the room, but it quickly dissipated.

My heart beat very fast; it had all seemed so real. Once again, my body was clammy with sweat. I got up, put on another nightgown and left the wet one on the floor before going back to bed. I lay awake for a very long time before I finally fell asleep.

The next morning, I awoke and looked around for Irene's diary. It had fallen to the floor and was upside down, completely open, its spine cracked. I picked it up and the entry was almost the last one.

> *That young girl, the pretty one in the cast came to see me today. She claimed to be my child, the one I left with Roger. I know it has to be true because her face is like looking at a picture of myself at that age. I told her otherwise. I cannot have a child appear in my life now. It is unacceptable. I won't have her interfere with my plans. She's lived this long on her own; she certainly doesn't need me now. She wants to get to know me, she says, but I'll wager she wants money. She'll get none from me and I told her so. She says she really wants what I have—a name for herself in the theater—making her own way and her own money—I could help her—could let her be my protégé and help her get roles. It will be a cold day in hell when I help her. What is this Mary Cosgrove to me? An inconvenience at the time and a nuisance now. I had to do everything on my own—had to create Irene Davenport and make her into what she is. No one ever helped me. I hate Chicago because it always reminds me of my past—let her make all the claims she wants—who*

will believe her? She can do what she will, but I will not help her.

I almost dropped the diary. Mary was Irene Davenport's daughter!

But how could Irene have been so heartless as to reject her? I thought about this for a long time. It made me consider my own life with my family. Suddenly, I was able to appreciate my parents' perspective—their love and fear for a daughter who wanted something so out of the ordinary, so unusual and unacceptable to them.

They might be angry with me, they might keep my brothers away from me and my father might argue with me whenever we meet, but would they really reject me flat out as Irene did? Would they really abandon me to my own devices? Would they? No. In my heart, I knew it was true. They loved me. I loved them. We were connected by that love and no matter what happened, no matter what I did to bend that bond, it would remain unbroken. What would it be like not to have that? Suddenly, I felt very sorry for Mary. Her mother—regardless of what kind of mother she had been—had rejected her. How incredibly hard that must have been for Mary.

That thought haunted me the rest of the day. I decided I had to do something to help Mary, to make things right in some way for her. I decided to go early to the theater, find her, and begin to repair our friendship. When I came in, I saw that Teddy wasn't at his desk. And then, I heard voices—male voices—on the stage. Jack Martin and Edward Hearne were arguing.

"It was you, I know it was you," Jack yelled.

"My dear boy, I have no idea to what you are referring."

Edward turned away from him, moving toward the stairs that led down to the dressing rooms.

"It was your fault. You killed my brother!"

Edward turned back to Jack, a shocked look on his face.

"What you suggest is preposterous!"

Jack took a step closer to him and I could see they were almost the same height, but their builds were very different—Edward was slim and lithe where Jack was solid and muscular. He looked Mr. Hearne directly in the face.

"He told me what you wanted. What you offered."

Edward paled, but stood his ground. "Then he misunderstood and I believe you are under a misconception."

"And when he wouldn't give it to you, you took it and killed him."

"Your brother was adorable, but a little young for my taste."

"From what I hear, you can't get them young enough."

"You hear incorrectly."

Jack raised his fist and hit Edward, catching him right on the jaw, causing him to stagger back, but he did not fall down.

Infuriated, Edward raised his cane and struck Jack in his midsection. He immediately bent over and hit the floor. Edward wielded the cane like a sword, and Jack didn't have a chance against Edward's years of experience in stage fighting. Jack tried to get out of the way but Edward struck Jack again and again.

I did not know what to do. I looked around for something or someone to help stop them. Just then, Mary ran in from the other side of the stage and stood in front of Jack. She screamed at them.

"Stop it, stop it! What's wrong with you two?"

Through extreme effort, Edward was able to bring himself under control and he lowered his stick.

"He killed Bobby!" Jack yelled.

Mary looked up at Edward in shock.

"I would never have hurt Bobby," Edward said, enunciating each of his words. "I had nothing to do with the death of that boy. Ask your boss, ask Roger Plant. He knows where I was after the performance that night."

He turned on his heel and exited off the stage moving right past me, down the stairs to his own dressing room. We all heard the door slam and the sound echoed in the empty theater.

Mary and I helped Jack up and onto a chair. I ran for some water and a compress. Jack was bruised very badly, but there did not seem to be any broken bones.

Mary talked to him as she dabbed his cheek.

"What were you thinking? Edward would never do such a thing. If you were thinking right, you would have known that."

"We both know somebody killed Bobby and I'm going to find out who and when I do, he will pay."

Jack got up and walked out of the theater slightly dragging his left leg behind him. Mary and I watched him go. Then, she threw the rag she had been using on Jack into the bucket of water.

"Men!" she said.

I added something about how stubborn and annoyingly single-minded they were. She laughed at that and James Jr. and his own single-mindedness flitted through my mind.

She wrung out the rag and I took a deep breath.

"Mary, can I talk to you for a few minutes?" I asked.

"I really think I should go see Edward and smooth his feathers before he drinks himself into incoherence before tonight's performance."

Her words were rather sharp, but there was a smile in her eyes and I took it as an invitation. I didn't know quite what to say about that, still not quite sure what had transpired with Edward. Innocent as I was in those days, I couldn't understand at all why Jack hated Edward or why Edward would be interested in Bobby Martin.

I wanted to make sure she didn't avoid me and so I said, "Well, later then. I found Irene's diary and she wrote about the play and some of the people and I wanted to ask you about it."

Mary looked at me curiously.

"Irene kept a diary?"

We heard Teddy's voice shout at that moment.

"What in the name of God's green earth is going on in my theater? Who is fighting? None of the scenery better be broken or there will be consequences."

Teddy strode in and it ended our conversation. At that point, I realized the theater was quite an emotional place; people let their feelings be known on a variety of topics and at the drop of a hat.

Mary simply said that Jack and Mr. Hearne had had a misunderstanding. Jack left and Mr. Hearne was probably nursing his feelings in his dressing room.

"I'll just go down there and see what I can do," she said.

"You do that, Miss."

Mary moved off down the stairs to the dressing rooms and Teddy turned to me.

"And now, Miss Nolan, perhaps you can explain to me exactly what happened."

"Well, Mr. Martin was under the impression that Mr. Hearne killed his brother. I believe he was seeking retribution."

"Ah, I see."

He looked at me. "Mr. Hearne is, at heart, a kind man. He has certain proclivities, but they don't involve boys. Do you understand me?"

Again, I really had no idea at the time what he meant, but he was so serious and so intent that I could only nod. He seemed satisfied with that and he left me to go about his business.

It all brought up so many more questions than answers. I wasn't making any progress on any level. Irene must have disagreed with me. That night, as I stood backstage and gritted my teeth in order to prepare myself to do my very best as the driven Lady Macbeth, I felt that familiar lightness. Irene was at hand, ready, perhaps even willing, to fulfill her part of the bargain. Once more, I felt myself rise up and out of my body. I had a momentary awareness of floating somewhere in the upper recesses of the fly space of the theater and then, my memory faded and I only recall a sense of peacefulness. It was obvious from the applause later that Irene had outdone herself.

It only encouraged me further to have my conversation with Mary. If I was going to have any kind of future, I needed friends in the theater. I knew in my heart that friends were created through shared experiences. The next day, we had a matinee. Afterwards, I changed my clothes and saw that Mary had done the same. She had her hat on and I saw her walk towards the stage door. I stopped her and told her I wanted to thank her for taking care of Mr. Hearne. She said that I didn't need to thank her, but she couldn't talk with me now as she had an errand to run. And then she rushed out the door.

It was clear to me that Edward was a very sensitive man. Cora had told me those with talent also suffered a burden of sensitivity. Certainly, that was the case with Mr. Hearne, but also, I felt, with Irene. In her diary, she seemed to massage every perceived injury and never made any reference to the many reviews or comments of her talent or brilliance. There were certainly enough of those over the years, but for some reason she never mentioned them. I began to feel sorry for her in a way I never expected.

I began to think of those I had met and worked with— they all seemed to have their secrets. Mr. Hearne and his drinking and whatever else drove him to it. It occurred to me that I never really saw him go onstage without access to some form of alcohol. He was always completely sober in the afternoons, but by the time an audience appeared, he seemed incapable of handling it unless he could drink his way through it.

Irene never truly appreciated herself or her talent and was constantly on the watch for some other person looking to take what she had or destroy her in some way. Mary and her jealousy over my winning the role of Lady Macbeth— how far would she go to destroy our friendship if indeed there was anything left? Certainly, this extended to Mrs. O'Neill and her compulsion to protect everything that had anything to do with Irene Davenport. It was almost as if Irene was still alive for her. Even Teddy was overly sensitive when it concerned his many superstitions. The only one who appeared to have any sense of normalcy had been Bobby Martin. He appeared to me just who and what he was—a young boy trying to do his best at his first real job. And now, he was dead. Why?

And what of the mysterious Roger Plant? Who was he and had he anything to do with Irene while she was in Chicago? If he was Mary's father and Jack's employer, was that their connection to one another? His name kept popping up and I wondered if he had some role in all of this? I had no idea who he was other than the fact that Jack worked for him and Edward knew him.

Among all of this, I could not discount an examination of the role I played, as well. Consumed in my desire to act, I had allowed Irene to possess my body on stage. In my own way, I was no better or worse than any of those whose motives I examined. Perhaps I was well fit for a life in the theater. A life of artifice. It was a sobering thought that I had a choice in front of me to go on as Irene's puppet or become my own person. I found I loved being in the theater and every experience—whatever it brought—only underlined my passion for it. Each performance was an adventure. The ritual of costume and make-up was comforting and natural to me. I loved being backstage waiting for an entrance, the excitement starting to pulse through my veins. I loved the interaction, the sense that, for a short time, this was my community of people gathered for a single purpose.

The only part I did not like was being on stage because I had no memory of what occurred there. I allowed Irene to have that experience. I knew I had to get it back, no matter what my potential was. I wanted my future, whether it would be as a star or just a walk on part. I had to know the length and breadth of my own abilities. That meant, I had to get rid of Irene. I had to find out who killed her. And, in my heart, I knew that whoever killed Irene had also murdered Bobby. They were connected in some way I just could not wrap my mind around. The killer had deliberately chosen Irene's pin to murder Bobby; it was thought out, the weapon acquired ahead of time. The circle part of the pin had not been found, which meant the murderer either still had it or had gotten rid of it.

My head ached with all the possibilities. How was I going to solve this? Did I know anything? Could I really do anything? I decided to look through Irene's diary. I would finish it and see if I could understand anything else or if there was any more information I could glean from it. I took my purse from the top of my dressing table where I had left it and opened it, only to discover the diary was gone.

Threescore and ten I can remember well;
Within the volume of which time I have seen
Hours dreadful and things strange, but this sore night
Hath trifled former knowings.

Macbeth Act II, Scene 4

〰〰〰〰〰〰〰〰〰〰〰〰〰〰〰〰〰〰〰〰〰

CHAPTER TEN

Chicago is a city of extremes.

One such extreme was a three-block area which ran along Fifth Avenue and was called Conley's Patch. Amazingly, it was just a few blocks from the courthouse and four blocks from the shops on State Street. The most notorious part of Conley's Patch was an area called Roger's Barracks. It was almost completely underground, a maze of tunnels and caves filled with criminals, gambling rooms and brothels. It was an indescribably horrible place—dark, corrupt and evil. It was referred to as the "Underworld," and was known to most citizens of Chicago as a place to avoid.

However, as a sheltered upper-class girl, I had no idea this world even existed. But, I was about to become very familiar with it soon after I discovered the theft of Irene's diary.

I knew Mary had taken the diary because she was the only person to whom I had mentioned its existence. I searched my dressing room thoroughly to see if I had misplaced it. It was nowhere to be found. Anger welled up in the pit of my stomach. Mary had stolen the diary! I was tired of being polite and easy-going. It was obvious Irene hadn't treated her very well, but I didn't care. She had violated my privacy and stolen from me! I had extended my friendship over and over and had been rebuffed and I wanted to know why. I walked out of the dressing room and almost collided with Teddy.

"Do you know where Mary went?" I demanded.

"No." he said, startled. "She just mentioned she had something important to do."

Without a word, I ran past him up the steps to the stage floor and out the door. I looked down Monroe Street and saw that she was walking down the street, just a block or so ahead. I had to move quickly if I was going to catch up with her.

It was another hot day, the air was very still and there were dried leaves scattered everywhere along the sidewalks and the street. There was a faint smell of smoke in the air, as there had been a fire the night before not very far from the theater, but I disregarded it. I was intent on catching up with Mary, confronting her and retrieving the diary. I hurried after her, but she continued to remain a block or so away from me. She never looked back, not once, and I could tell how focused she was on getting wherever she was going. As we moved down Monroe, she

turned left on Fifth Avenue and the area quickly
deteriorated in appearance. The shops were dirtier, the
few houses were dilapidated or abandoned and the people
on the sidewalk were not very well-dressed and they
stared at me. But, I didn't care, as I was completely
focused. She stopped and when I did, an old woman
bumped into me.

"Watch it there," she said.

I murmured an apology, but looked on as Mary turned
the corner on Adams. I hurried to catch up and saw Mary
walk into what looked like the most decrepit building I had
ever seen. A small voice inside me suggested that perhaps it
was time to go back to the theater, but I ignored it and
crossed the street to the doorway where Mary had
disappeared. There was a sign above it that spelled out
"O'Malley" in broken letters and I pushed the door open
and walked in.

It was the first saloon I had ever been in and I
wondered if they were all so disgusting. There were very
few customers, none of whom were interested in me. A
large man stood behind the bar, a dirty apron tied around
his rotund waist.

"What you want, girlie?"

I was taken aback for a moment and I had to summon
all my courage just to simply say, "I'm here for Mary
Cosgrove."

"Mm," he grunted and gestured with his head toward
a doorway to the right of the bar. I went and opened the
door; it led to a stairway that went down and down and
down. The heat and smell of too many bodies enclosed in
too small a space rose up, but I just thought that if this was

something Mary could face, then so could I. And, down I went.

I soon found myself in another world. It appeared I had found the Chicago that Jack had referred to. This was the Underworld—or the part of it known as Roger's Barracks after Roger Plant.

At the bottom of the stairs stood a woman who appeared to be in her late forties and was slovenly dressed. Her hair was mostly gray and quite disheveled. She was surrounded by four or five little girls. One of them was wearing torn clothing and all of them were filthy. Several had no shoes. The woman had a purse in her hand and was going through the contents. Whatever she saw seemed to please her.

"Good job, Alice," she said, "The rest of you see what Alice has brought me? "

Then, she noticed me.

"Well, look what we have here. Who might you be?

"I'm with—meeting Mary Cosgrove."

"Are you now? Any of you girls see Mary?"

Four of them looked at me, and then glanced back at her. None of them said a word, but the youngest chose to speak.

"I saw her. She went to see–"

Before she could say more, she got her cheek slapped with a force that almost sent her to the ground.

"What did you say?" the woman said in an even voice.

"Nothing."

"That's right."

"Here, we only give information if the price is right. What are you offering?"

I felt as if I had stepped down the rabbit hole from Lewis Carroll's book, *Alice's Adventures In Wonderland*. The whole place was surreal, but I knew if I didn't offer something, I would not get the information I wanted. I didn't usually carry much money with me. Then I remembered. I did have some money to pay for the cabs that took me back and forth to Grandmother's. Perhaps she would be satisfied with that.

I was about to get some money out of my purse when the woman took a step toward me. The girls, except for the smallest one who had drawn back, followed her lead and surrounded me. One of them touched my dress lovingly, leaving a dry, dusty smudge.

"I'm afraid I don't have very much."

"Well, let's just see..." and she grabbed my purse out of my hand. Before I could protest, she expertly lifted every cent I had from it. I made a move to go and retreat back up the stairs, but one of the older girls was already standing there now, leaning against the banister, an awful look upon her face.

Then, the woman laughed in a particularly unattractive way. As hot as it was down there, I felt a chill go right down my backbone and into my stomach.

"You come with me. I'll show you where Mary went."

I decided to push my way back up the stairs past the girl when the woman grabbed me by the arm and dragged me through a doorway.

The world into which I stepped felt surreal and sinister at the same time. She force-marched me through room after room, some empty and in some, people lay on cots, unconscious, and I wondered if they were dead. In others, people were drinking and playing cards. Very soon, I had no idea of the direction or a sense of where I was or how I had gotten there. I couldn't have found my way back with a map. We kept moving and she finally came into a place where a number of women were—they were all barely dressed and looked worn and tired. A woman who looked even older and harder than the one who held my arm so tightly sat at a small desk, reading a book. I immediately recognized it as Irene's small leather bound diary and knew that Mary had indeed been here. She looked up as we approached.

"Well, Sally. What have you got for me?"

"A very pretty little fly walked smack into our web, Ann."

Ann closed the book and came over to me. She was tall, her clothing was more expensive than the woman who held on to me and she had an air of command about her. She held up my chin, and then walked around me.

"Something special," she said, softly.

I spoke up.

"I'm looking for Mary Cosgrove. She's a friend of mine. Is she here now?"

"Well, you won't find her here—she's gone, bought herself out, in a manner of speaking. Don't suppose you can do the same?"

Both women found this incredibly amusing and cackled together over their shared humor.

I thought of *Macbeth* and screwing my courage to the sticking place, so I said, "I don't know what is so funny."

At least that stopped their laughter.

"You are, my sweet. Welcome to hell."

Again, they laughed, finding themselves infinitely amusing.

"Make yourself comfortable. Sit down and I'll be right with you," Ann said.

I took stock of my surroundings and found I was being watched by the other, younger women who were sitting around as if they were waiting for something to happen. The two women conferred and Ann drew a bundle of money from her bodice, peeled off a number of bills and handed them over to Sally, who nodded and left.

Then, Ann turned to me and said, with a smile that was not reflected in her eyes, "You cost me a pretty penny, but I think you'll be worth it."

She walked over to me, reached out her hand and ripped the bodice of my dress straight down to my waist. Outraged, I tried to hit her across the face, but she punched me in the head so hard that in the next moment, I knew nothing.

I dreamt that I stood in the middle of the Illinois and Michigan Central Depot station. I watched a young girl walk out of one of the train terminals. She was around fifteen or sixteen, inexpensively dressed and she carried a cheap suitcase with her. She reminded me a lot of Mary. She walked aimlessly around the train station, in some awe of the place. She looked fresh and pretty and wholesome. I sensed and knew immediately it was a much younger version of Irene. I watched as the horrible woman who had hit me came over to her. She was younger, too, and dressed simply as a working woman. She smiled at Irene and engaged her in a conversation.

"No!" I cried. But, Irene couldn't hear me.

"What's your name, dear?"

And Irene said, "Margaret Conklin."

"Margaret, that's lovely. Is someone meeting you?"

"No. I'm here to look for work. I heard you could make as much as three dollars a week as a maid in a hotel in Chicago."

"That's very true. Why don't you let me help you? It's my job to find work for girls like you—girls new to the city. Will you let me help you?"

"Really? You'll help me?"

"I know all the hotels in Chicago—which ones are hiring new maids and what they pay."

They walked out of the train station together and the next thing I knew, Irene was in a dark room and her clothes were gone and there were large, dark figures surrounding her. She was screaming and a man's voice said roughly, "Get off, let me have a go at her."

And she screamed and screamed and it was the screaming that woke me up.

I came to in a very dark, very small room. I had no idea how much time had passed. My head ached and I was incredibly thirsty. I sat up, but that was a mistake. The darkness moved and swam around me. I clasped my head with both hands, as if that would make the room stop.

It was then I realized that my clothes were gone and I was dressed only in my chemise. *My god, where am I,* I asked myself. *What have I gotten myself into?* My first inclination was to panic. No one knew that I was here. Mary didn't even know I had followed her and certainly Teddy didn't know where I went. What would happen when I didn't show up at the theater? Would an alarm be set? Would anybody look for me? How would they even know where to look? And my parents! Oh my god—and Grandmother—what would they do when I didn't come back? What had I done to them? What if I never saw them again? I wanted to throw myself back on the cot and weep.

Panic began to spread through every bone and sinew of my body. As I looked around the room, a deep visceral fear expanded and became a great gnawing beast that all but overcame me. I was in the very same room from my dream, the room in which Irene had been attacked.

I couldn't think, I couldn't feel. The fear came on me so quickly and so completely that it overwhelmed my every sense and froze me in place. And then, I heard a small, insistent voice in my head saying, "Get out."

My mind wrapped around those two words and they reverberated though my brain. They became louder and more emphatic, "Get out, get out, get out!"

In the next moment, the temperature in the room dropped and the chill caused the sweat on my body to congeal. Irene. Irene was here now. I felt her with every fiber of my being. She was here with me. A wave of deep emotion swept over me and I knew it was anger on a level I had never experienced before. She was furious and it began to burn in me as well. I began to feed upon it. Her anger, her hatred originated in this place and I knew she hated everyone here. I felt that white hot anger coil around me and run through my core.

I stood up. I was barefoot, but didn't care. I went over to the door and found there was no handle. I was completely locked in. The anger pulsed and wracked over my body. I beat on the door. I heard Ann's laughter from the other side.

"Ah, you're awake! Anxious for your first customers, are you?"

I beat on the door again. I heard only laughter.

That laughter fed my outrage, which in turn, seemed to fuel Irene's presence. I backed away, looking for a chair, something, anything, to pick up and throw at the door. Irene moved in front of me. I could feel her energy beat and burn, the level of her fury creating dim pulses of shadow in the dark room. The door started to shake, warp and then all at once, blew off of its hinges and exploded into the outer room.

Ann stood there, shock and surprise written plainly on her face. I paused in the doorway and I could sense Irene in front of me, moving toward Ann.

"What the hell?" Ann shouted.

The chair, the table, the small desk, the lamp all started to tip and rock as I walked forward. The other women in the room immediately scattered and disappeared into the rabbit warren of tunnels around us, but Ann held her ground.

Irene. It was all Irene. It was so cold now, so very cold. A mist rose in the air in front of me and coalesced into an indistinct form. The freezing air spread out in front of me.

I continued walking forward. I could tell Ann felt the cold, too. Her breath came out in clouds. She was speechless, her face a mask of fear. Irene's diary was still in Ann's hand and, as I focused upon it, a stream of cold air blasted directly at her, forcing her backward and throwing her onto the floor. The diary flew up into the air, straight at me and I caught it.

Ann turned an even paler shade of white and screamed. She picked herself up and headed straight at me. In my mind, I heard a voice—it was Irene's—and it said, "Run."

I dodged around her and took off, not knowing where I was going, but moving. Ann followed behind screaming at others to help her, screaming at me to stop, but I ran as fast as I could. Without the inconvenience of my dress, I ran as if my life depended upon it and I knew that it did. I had no idea which way to go to get out of this maze, but Irene knew. She whispered to me.

"Left…right…straight now…"

I didn't think, I just went, with Ann following, screaming at me for all she was worth.

Very soon, I recognized the staircase to the saloon and I knew I was almost free. Just up those stairs and out into bar and then out onto the street and I knew I would be safe. I made for the stairs and was about to climb them when a man stepped off the last step and stood in front of me. He was a very small man, thin and wiry, extremely well-dressed. Despite his size, his very presence was enough for me to feel his power. I felt around for Irene's fury, but it had dissipated, softened and then was gone all together. I was alone once more and felt all my energy drain away.

"And who's this then?" he asked.

For one brief moment, I thought this man would save me. Just then Ann caught up to me and tried to grab me roughly by the elbow.

"She belongs to me," Ann said.

"Oh really, she doesn't look like one of your regular types."

"This one's different."

Panic rose in my throat. This wasn't my savior at all, he was merely curious and he was completely blocking my way.

"I've paid for her alright, as Sally will testify."

He seemed bored with that answer and merely nodded at Ann. She pulled my arm so hard I knew there would be a bruise.

I heard more footsteps come down the stairs and, at that moment, I knew I was well and truly lost. I was completely deserted by Irene and there was no one here who could possibly help me. And then, I heard my name.

"Lillian?"

At first, I thought I had imagined it and then, I heard a familiar voice.

"What in the name of all that's holy are you doing here?"

Jack Martin stood behind and above the small man in front of him.

It was nothing less than a miracle. Jack Martin had appeared as if out of nowhere and I was saved.

"What's your interest in this, Jack?" the man asked.

"She was a friend of Bobby's. She was helping him learn to read, Mr. Plant."

So this was Roger Plant. I heard a whisper and then, a sigh.

"Oh, how did she come to be here, then?"

His face changed, now curious once again.

I found my voice.

"A mistake," was all I could manage.

I could read a good deal of caution in Jack's face as I looked over Roger Plant's shoulder. Mr. Plant found this uproariously funny, for some reason.

"A mistake. Well, that's for sure now. A mistake, indeed. Since she's a friend of yours, you take her, Jack."

"What?" screamed Ann. "She cost me! She's mine."

"Shut it, woman."

I was amazed when she backed off. Mr. Plant came down and looked at me. It was at that moment, I felt Irene again. And she whispered, *"You always had one small, soft spot in that cold heart."*

Jack's startled face told me that I had actually said the words out loud. Those who had gathered around to watch the show went dead quiet.

"Irene?" Mr. Plant asked.

His face was white and a trickle of sweat coursed down his right cheek.

Get out now, was all that floated across my mind and I moved slowly by Mr. Plant, up to Jack, past him and up the stairs. Jack turned and followed right behind me all the way. There were many more patrons at the bar now and several of them leered at me and would have made a move had Jack not stood directly behind me. He whipped off his suit jacket.

"Put this on, you're practically naked."

I slipped into his jacket, slightly damp with his sweat, but ever so grateful for the cover.

"Now, how in the hell am I going to get you out of here?"

He went out the door to the curb and I quickly followed. A very seedy cab pulled by an ancient horse was coming down the street and Jack whistled for him. He hustled me in, turned to me and demanded to know exactly how I ended up in a whorehouse in Roger's Barracks when I finally burst into tears.

Jack sighed and put his arm around me, patting me on the shoulder. It was lovely. I felt completely safe and so I wept on and on. It was as if every drop of moisture was being wrung from my body and came out through my eyes. Every emotion that I had felt during the course of that horrible adventure churned through my body and I began to shake. As I wept, he began to rock me, saying incomprehensible, but soothing words, soft words that were only sounds for me, words that had no meaning, but were healing in their sentiment. It was only a short way to the theater, but I wasn't finished crying when we got there.

"We're at the theater. Is this where you want to go or shall I take you to your Grandmother's?" he asked.

The thought of Grandmother jerked me out of my tears. She must never know; no one must ever know what happened to me today or she would certainly remove all her support and I would be back at home before I knew it and I would never set foot in a theater again.

"No. I don't want her to see me like this."

I wiped my eyes with the back of my hand.

"I'm better," I said. "I'm alright. Thank you, Jack. You saved my life."

I smiled up into those crystal blue eyes and, for a moment, I felt lost in their depths.

"Well, I wouldn't say that exactly. You did a pretty good job yourself—no one's ever escaped Ann's clutches before."

He took his arm away and that startled me back into myself. I took a deep breath and was about to get out of the cab when he grabbed my arm.

"What on earth were you doing there, Lillian?"

"It's a long story, Jack and I can't talk about it right now. But I will. I think I'm beginning to understand about what's happened at the theater. Did you know Irene came from Roger's Barracks?"

"There were rumors, but it was before I started working for Mr. Plant."

"What do you mean? How old was Irene?"

He laughed.

"All I know is Ann has many ways to recruit young girls for her brothel. She tells them she can get them a respectable job at a hotel or as a housemaid. Then she leads them to the Underworld and…"

Obviously my reaction to this horrible story gave him pause because he finished abruptly.

"And then they are ruined and there is no way to get a respectable job after that. Mary has this theory that Irene came from the Underworld and that Roger was the one to get her out. I don't believe it myself. The Roger I know would never do anything like that.

"Story was she was one of the girls Ann 'recruited' and ruined. Irene came down to Chicago from some small farm town. Ann uses the train station as a hunting ground for new girls and she snapped Irene right up with the promise of a job. Irene was ruined and there was no way she could get a respectable job after that. No choice other than to become a whore. There was never any love lost between those two. She wanted out bad—who wouldn't? She was working for Ann when Roger saw her. She was always pretty and he claimed her for himself. No one ever challenges him. He rules down there. That was her first step out."

"Perhaps he loved her!"

Jack laughed again.

"As if he is capable—no, but if Mary's story is true then he must have had a weakness for her."

"A soft spot," I whispered.

"What? Oh yes, and I'm sure it cost her though. Roger never does anything for free. No matter how soft a spot he might have had for her, she would have had to pay him back."

He paused and became thoughtful.

"Roger loves money more than anything. He helped me get Bobby the job at the theater and it's still costing me. I wanted to protect him. Lot of good that did."

"You couldn't protect him from what happened. Jack, I think—I know Irene was murdered and Bobby saw something and he was killed, too. You couldn't have saved him."

"Irene's death was accidental. The police said so."

"Her pearls were wired, not strung. They didn't break when they caught on the scenery—she just hung there, remember?"

"My God, and you think Bobby had something to do with it?"

"No. I think he got in the way somehow or he saw something. I don't know how or what."

He was quiet for a moment and then, I asked him, "I followed Mary there today—what do you think she was doing there?"

His whole demeanor changed, softened.

"I've known her since she was a kid. She grew up in the Underworld."

"That horrible place?"

"Funny thing when I think about it. Roger got her out. She was supposed to work for Ann when she turned thirteen, but Roger stepped in and got her a job in a theater, always in Chicago. She's been working here for the past five years."

"She's close to my age?"

"How old did you think she was?"

"She seemed older—not in looks, exactly, but experience."

"Roger's Barracks will do that to you."

I almost blurted out that I had found out that Mary was Irene's daughter. If that were true, it was likely that Roger must be her father. But I had to read the rest of the diary before I said anything to Jack. The time was getting late and another problem occurred to me.

I looked up and asked, "Jack, do you think you can you get me in without being seen?"

"It's early yet," he said. "I think I can manage it."

It was unbelievable to me that so much had happened in such a short amount of time. Jack had the driver pull right up to the alley, got me down and got me in, past

Teddy's post and down the stairs to my dressing room. I gave him back his jacket.

He turned to walk out just as Mrs. O'Neill came in and she narrowed her eyes, but she didn't say anything and he quickly left. I could feel her disproval, but I had been through way too much to regard it. I felt filthy and wanted to clean myself.

I turned to her and said, "I'd love a bath. Can you get some water for me, Mrs. O'Neill?"

She stalked out and I sat down on the chaise, exhausted. I had wedged the diary into my waistband along my back and now remembered it was there. I don't know why I didn't tell Jack about the diary—I wanted to keep it to myself a while longer, I suppose. I pulled it out and flipped through it.

I began to think about Irene and Mary and what their lives had been like. Feelings and images floated across my mind. I now understood how Irene withdrew into herself, how she eventually developed the resolve to figure a way out. I felt I could almost see her waiting, watching for an opportunity. She must have learned to act by allowing her physical appearance to belie what was going inside of her, as if she could be two separate people at the same time. An image came to mind as I saw Roger Plant through her eyes. She must have immediately noticed the interest he had taken in her and recognized that she could have power through influence. I could imagine Ann's rage as Roger took Irene away from her.

Images started to come faster. I could see Irene in nice clothes, much cleaner and fresh. Once again, I heard the words, *"Soft spot in a cold heart"* and I know these were words Irene had once spoken to Roger. I then sensed Irene's pregnancy, the birth of the child, her pain, her exhaustion. The vision shifted and I saw Irene dressed in street clothes. I watched her as she walked up the stairs to the saloon and Roger stood below. A tall, thin woman appeared from the shadows next to him holding the baby girl, now almost a year old, in her arms. I could not see the woman's face, but there was something familiar about her.

Irene didn't look back and the picture faded. The scene shifted again, and it was like looking at different dramatizations of the same play. Irene standing backstage, always watching, watching. Irene, as she looked out at the audience, one stage after another, different costumes, different places. I heard applause. It became stronger and stronger, and I felt how Irene fed on it. Finally, I saw Irene onstage as Lady Macbeth.

She glanced over across the stage and looked straight at me—she held a bouquet of yellow roses and then, I knew I could no longer watch. I tried to pull away, but I could feel her forcing me to watch, forcing me to go through her death. We were connected and I could not break that bond. The scenery started to move and Irene's pearls caught on it. I could feel them tighten around her neck—my neck. I was the one being strangled. I started to gasp for breath and I felt as if I was going to faint when the door banged open and Mrs. O'Neill entered with two buckets of water. The vision quickly dissipated and was gone.

"I had to go all the way down the street for the water."

I slipped the diary under the seat of my chair. I never wanted to touch it again. I took a deep, cleansing breath.

"Thank you, Mrs. O'Neill. I'll take it from here."

She put the water down and walked out. I got up, stripped off my chemise and threw it in the trash. I took a sponge and the soap she left with it and began to wash myself. The water was warm and soothing and I started to feel more like myself as I washed away the dirt and grime of the Underworld.

My thoughts turned to my own life. Having been raised in an environment of love and protection, I had just assumed everyone else had the same experience. Life had been very different for Irene and Mary. It didn't seem possible to me that both existences could go on at the same time in the same city. Only a few short blocks from here, women my age were being used and abused as I sat in a dressing room of one of the best theaters in the city and prepared to perform a major role in a Shakespearean play, produced by one of the most powerful men in theater. It was all too much to think about.

As I cleaned my body, I attempted to clean away my thoughts. One thing I knew was that Irene was becoming a more powerful influence over me. I believed that she no longer just wanted to possess my body during the play— she wanted my life. I was in danger of losing myself if I didn't break the connection to her…and yet, I was drawn to her and what she had, who she was. I also felt gratitude for her part in my rescue from that horrible place.

I finished with my bath and felt so much better. As I began to dress for the performance, I looked around the room and realized I had done nothing to make it my own. Irene's trunks, her portrait, all of her possessions were scattered about. I began to pick them up and put them away in her trunks. The tartan shawl was draped over the chaise lounge, so I picked it up, folded it around the diary—being quite careful not to touch the book again as I wound the fabric around it. I tucked the whole thing deep into the side of the trunk and closed the lid. The room was neater now and much less cluttered. I pushed all her possessions into the furthest corner of the room as far from me as possible and left them there.

I sat down in front of the mirror and began to put on my make-up and arrange my hair for that evening's performance. I decided that no matter what, Irene was never going to have possession of my body again. If I had to give up being Lady Macbeth, so be it. I was going to have to anyway when Mr. Daly replaced me. But, more than that, I wanted my own life in the theater. I wanted to succeed or fail on my own. I knew I had some ability, but I had just let Irene take over. I was not the same girl I had been just a week ago.

That night, Irene and I engaged in a struggle for control. It was war with her and she threw everything at her disposal into it. The performance became a constant battle between us. I could feel Irene's presence, her need and hunger to take over my body and it was almost overwhelming. Every time I felt the lightness, I pulled myself back in, forced myself to stay focused in my body and, in the present moment. Mary Cosgrove stood in the wings and watched and I felt her eyes on me at all times. But, I could not think about her as I had to completely concentrate on what I was doing.

The performance must have appeared incredibly disjointed to the audience. The mad scene in particular was done differently than it had ever been done before and it certainly had new meaning for me! I was so relieved when it was over, as it was my last appearance in the role that night, but was amazed by the applause I received. At that moment, I knew what it was like to be in a role and be responsible for that role. I finally knew what it was to be an actress. I had done it myself, without Irene and with the realization that her power over me was broken. I knew the war was not over with Irene, but I had won this battle.

As I bowed to the audience, a large bouquet of roses was brought to me by Thomas, the new call boy. I leaned across the edge of the stage and he handed them up to me. As the lights were in my eyes, I could not tell, at first, the hue or color of the roses. They were heavy with a deep, fragrance, and as I gathered them into my arms, I saw they were yellow.

It flashed through my mind that Irene had received yellow roses the night she died. There was no card, but I was convinced Mary had sent them to me as a warning

I turned and walked off the stage. Teddy was there to meet me. He immediately took the bouquet from me and threw them into the waste can by his office. But, instead of making some dire prediction about their presence in the theater, he surprised me when he said, "Good girl, you won that round, but Irene's still here. You're going to have to get rid of her all together."

Thriftless ambition, that will ravin up
Thine own life's means!

Macbeth Act II, Scene 4

~~~~~~

CHAPTER ELEVEN

After the performance was over, I was exhausted. It was an effort to walk down the stairs to my dressing room where I collapsed on the chaise lounge. I knew I was in control now, but I was still on guard as Irene's presence danced along the edge of my mind. However, I had to completely exorcise her. I had to be free of her. Whatever the world beyond was, she needed to embrace it and become part of it; she needed to move on. I sensed that that was not going to be easy because she had unfinished business here. And I was the conduit to getting it done.

I sighed and sat up. I began to remove some of the pieces of my costume when there was a knock on the door.

"Come in," I said.

Mary Cosgrove walked in.

"Teddy said you were looking for me this afternoon."

I looked at Mary differently now. I had always felt she was so much older and wiser than me. I had felt inferior in some way because she had so much more experience. Now, my perspective was that our situations had reversed—I was the older, wiser, more experienced one and she, the initiate.

I had started out in our relationship trying to please her. Perhaps because this was something innate in my upbringing or perhaps it was just my personality that meant to please. I no longer felt that way. Mary never had any intention of ever trying to please me. I had a much better understanding of her now, who she was and what motivated her. My experiences throughout the day had created an older, wiser, more experienced Lillian Nolan *and* Rosemary Hampton. I knew things that she did not. But again, I misjudged her.

"Yes. I found you—or found where you went."

Her eyes widened at that, but she said nothing.

"Haven't you spoken with Jack?" I asked.

"Jack? What does Jack have to do with anything?"

"I know who you are and where you came from. I met Sally…and Ann."

I don't know what I expected, but I certainly did not expect her to laugh.

"So?" she said. "What difference does that make? By now, you should know an actress has the worst sort of reputation. Who else would show themselves on a stage so shamelessly? Now, you are one of us."

"That's not what I mean. Sit down."

She sat on the chair in front of my dressing table and once again, I thought about how angelic in appearance she was. Her eyes were a deep green and I remembered that they were just like Irene's. Mary's lovely blonde hair framed her exquisite face.

"I read your mother's diary."

There was a pause, almost as if time had stopped while she pondered this. Her expression did not change, but a shift occurred in her eyes.

"My mother," she spat out, and paused. "Irene Davenport was no mother. She may have given birth to me, but she left me in that place. Traded me, she told me—for her freedom. She got out, but she left me there."

She looked me in the eye.

"You have no idea what growing up in that hellhole was like. The only thing she ever gave me was the desire to get out. It consumed me. It wasn't until I learned that Roger Plant was my father—and that I was something unexpected—that I knew I had some kind of leverage. I knew he would never help me unless I could use that leverage in some way."

She got up and walked over to the portrait of Irene and pulled the dust cover off of it.

"Sally never knew. I used to go from store to store…learned to steal and not get caught. I was actually quite good at it. I would listen to the conversations of the women I stole from. I wanted that—I wanted to talk like them, be like them. I wanted their lives and so desperately to escape mine. So, I learned to speak properly and hide it. Those were my first acting lessons.

"Then, one day, I heard Roger arguing with Ann—she wanted me in her brothel. I must have been thirteen at the time. I knew what went on throughout the Underworld— knew every inch of it—it was my home, after all. But, I did not want to work for Ann. I saw the girls she brought in and what happened to them. Many died before they were sixteen, in horrible ways. I knew I could not go directly to Roger and ask for special treatment—he would no more admit he had fathered me than anyone else. So, I came up with a plan and went to him.

'Hear me out,' I said to Roger. 'I can be a maid at the Tremont Hotel and I'll pay fifty percent of my wages to you.'

"He wanted seventy percent—hardly anything left for me to live on…but then, he said a funny thing. He said, 'you can earn more at the theater. I know somebody, I'll set it up.' Of course, Ann was furious, but what Roger says goes and he is nothing else if not a greedy little man, but also one, I knew, who kept his word, especially when money was involved.

"So, I began an apprenticeship in the theater, working from house to house in Chicago—at Crosby's Opera House, at the McVickers Theater, even here at the Grand. And, I gave most of it to Roger. And I waited."

She looked up at the portrait.

"Then, Irene Davenport came to Chicago. She was so beautiful. She was everything I wanted to be. Men didn't use her, she used them and they worshipped her for it. I watched her, I followed her and I wanted to know everything about her. She was all I ever wanted.

"One day, when I was paying Roger my money, I must have said or done something to make him say, 'see the theater is rubbing off on you—you're just like that whore Davenport.'

'Never,' I said. 'She's not a whore.'

"He laughed at that and said, 'Sure she is. Just as you will be if you stop payment—like mother, like daughter.'

'What's that supposed to mean?' I asked him. 'She's the most beautiful, talented woman in the world.'

'She's your mother, girl, and she left you here.' That shut me up and he laughed again.

"I could barely believe it—Irene Davenport was my mother? I had to know for certain. I had to confront her. How do you accuse the woman, the woman who is everything you want to be, of abandoning you? In my heart, there was a small part that spoke to me and said, *if she truly is your mother, she will help you. She will see it in you and what you want and she will help you—she will acknowledge who and what you are.*

"After all my experiences, after all that, I still had hope. Some tiny spark in me believed that there was a chance that I could be recognized and maybe even accepted. Irene Davenport killed that hope. After rehearsal, I met her. I preyed upon her sensibilities and approached her as the humble servant to the master. She never saw it for the acting it was. I played to her vanity and was rewarded with a few moments of conversation.

"Then, I told her I knew she was my mother. I knew about Roger. I thought for a moment she understood, that we were connected because we had had the same experience. She had abandoned me, but, on some level, I understood and knew that if she acknowledged me, even if it was just between the two of us, it could be all right. She could help me to achieve what she did. She could help me to get out and away from Roger's Barracks."

Mary paused for a moment, her eyes beginning to water.

"I was so stupid," she continued. "Her whole countenance changed and her body shook with rage. She said she had no idea what I was talking about. Never heard of any Roger. Who did I think I was? She never bred any daughter. If I came near her again, she would have me fired, would have me blackballed from ever working in the theater again. She screamed at me and O'Neill came and threw me out. That was my mother. Everything I thought of, everything I felt for Irene died."

She began to move around the room, touching the trunks and various possessions of Irene's that were in the room.

"I used to pretend that my mother was someone very famous and rich and I had been taken from her and she didn't have any idea where I was or what had become of me. I'd pretend that she spent her days mourning my loss and her life was never the same, consumed in worry over what my fate had been. Instead, I met my mother that night and I learned that she cared nothing for me or what happened to me. She never gave me a thought. I wasn't even an inconvenience. I simply did not exist.

"I crawled into a deep hole that night and, for the first time in years, I cried for everything I had lost—including my future. Teddy found me the next morning and he called Jack. Jack came and took me away. It was the day before *Macbeth* opened and he got some food in me and let me sleep. I knew Jack had always been sweet on me and I let him take care of me."

Listening to her story, mesmerized by the depth and scope of it, I was unaware of a growing coldness in the room and I felt a shiver go down my spine.

Irene was here. I glanced in the mirror and saw a slight mist behind me start to form into the shape of Irene.

"Mary, you need to leave now."

She looked at me for a moment, having forgotten I was even in the room. She turned back to the portrait of Irene.

"The incomparable Irene Davenport," she said in a low voice. "I hope she's burning in hell."

As she stood looking at the portrait, I could see the resemblance—one dark, one light, but the same shape of face, the same turn of body, the same hands, the same eyes. She was indeed Irene's daughter.

"That's why I sabotaged the performance opening night. I deliberately put myself in the way of people making their cues—oh, not to make them too late, just to keep them off balance, to keep Irene off balance. I took some of the props and then, while everyone was frantically searching for them, replaced them. I made sure that Hearne's pitcher was pure alcohol rather than the usual dilution of water. I was the one that sent the yellow roses. I wanted to hurt her in the only place she cared about—her performance. I wanted to make her debut in Chicago a memorable one because it would be so horrible."

With those words, the energy in the room began to spin. Even Mary felt it and turned back toward me.

"Get out, Mary, get out. Irene is here."

Mary's eyes went wide and she backed up toward the door, flung it open and sprinted down the hallway. A howling sound arose, like the cry of a fierce wind through the trees. I watched as Mary ran for her life and disappeared up the stairs and away from Irene.

I felt so sorry for Mary. She only wanted what we all want—recognition from those that we respect. Irene's anger and spite knew no end. She was furious that Mary knew her secrets. She needed to let Mary go. Irene had done enough to her and I was caught in the middle of their personal tragedy and felt that I had to do something, but what? And, although Mary did not confess to killing Irene, was she the one responsible? Would she go that far? Had she strung Irene's pearls with wire and watched her mother twist and die?

Mary managed to get out of the theater and I heard the echo of the alley stage door slam all the way down to my dressing room.

*I would not have such a heart in my
bosom for the dignity of the whole body.*

Macbeth Act V, Scene 1

CHAPTER TWELVE

The next day was Sunday and the theater was dark. There
would be no performance. It was odd weather for early
October, as the conditions continued to be hot and dry.
During the performance last night, there had been another
fire in which four city blocks had been destroyed, but the
conflagration had been contained by the fire department.
When I awoke that morning, the odor of the smoke was in
the air again.

I will never forget how incredibly windy it was that
day. Even now, so many years later when I think about
that day, I can still feel it and smell it. Gusts blew through
and around the house and down the street that were so
strong that as Grandmother and I walked to church that
morning, the wind continually caught our dresses and we
almost lost our hats several times. The dust and the dirt

were everywhere, blowing through shades in windows and doorways, forming small piles.

Grandmother loved Sundays. She enjoyed going to church where she took particular pleasure in the sermons of Dr. Robert Collyer. He was one of the most famous clergymen in Chicago, had been an Abolitionist and during the War, had been a camp inspector for the Sanitary Commission. Grandmother still remembered the Sunday he notified the congregation that he was planning to join the fight. He walked in carrying a flag, draped it over the pulpit and announced, "This place is closed. I'm going to the war."

As we sat in church that morning, we could hear the sound of the wind, as well as the continual creaking of the limbs of the trees. Dr. Collyer's sermon was on the topic of forgiveness. My mind drifted to Irene and Mary. Were there some things that were unforgiveable? Was it possible for Mary to forgive Irene for what she had done to her—even after Irene's death? And what about Irene? She was consumed by her vengeance. What did she hope to achieve once her murderer was found? And what was the purpose—the satisfaction in that?

One phrase Dr. Collyer said that day has always stuck in my mind.

Not to forgive is a poison you give yourself and expect the other person to die.

I thought about how obsessed Irene was with revenge. Her life had been filled with blame and censure. Even now, she was reaching out from "the Beyond" to punish the person responsible for her death. She was incapable of forgiveness and it had eaten her life away.

Then, I had an epiphany of my own. What about my own life? My own family? What was I doing to create such dissension among those I had always loved? Was it possible that I could forgive—could they forgive me? I realized then that I had a lot of anger where my parents were concerned. That if I wasn't going to poison myself, I had to consider how to forgive them *and* still pursue the life I so wanted. What if they never forgave me? Could I carry that through my life?

After the service, Grandmother commented upon how quiet I had become, but I merely said that Dr. Collyer had given me a lot to think about. She seemed pleased that he had made such an impact upon me.

I was still determined to pursue an acting career. It felt so right, so true to me. I knew it was my destiny and I was meant to be an actress right down to the fiber of my being. Yet, the knowledge of the impact it had on those I loved weighed heavily on me. I could not forget Father's last words—that I was unforgiven. Where was my compassion and forgiveness and how was it to be communicated or offered? I did not have the answer. I knew I had to continue along my life's path, but I also knew I had to find some way to find peace with my family. At this juncture, I just could not see the way.

Grandmother and I shared a very quiet lunch at home after church that day. We agreed to cancel our plans for an excursion to the lakefront, as it was impossible to do anything outside with the wind as violent as it was. Grandmother decided a nap was in order and she retired to her bedroom to take full advantage of the change in plans.

I was very restless and decided to sit on the sofa in the front parlor and read. Grandmother was a fan of the writer Jules Verne and she had kept his books on the shelves near the fireplace. I picked up a copy of *All Around the Moon*, which had been published the previous year and was a sequel to *From the Earth to the Moon*, which had been published five years prior. The wind blew outside and occasionally the windows rattled. It was so quiet indoors that afternoon that I could clearly hear the ticking of the large grandfather clock in the foyer. The monotonous beat began to lull me to sleep. I yawned and plumped the pillows behind my back, swung my feet over and onto the sofa and crossed my ankles. I couldn't seem to keep my eyes open one more moment and it was not very long at all before I dropped the book on my chest and fell asleep almost immediately.

Once again, it seemed to me that I was not asleep at all. And then I heard a voice. I could not hear the exact words, but I definitely heard the murmur of someone speaking. It was low—not a whisper, but more like an undertone, a one-sided conversation. It was then that I knew I was truly asleep because I found myself backstage in the theater at the top of the stairs leading down to my dressing room below the stage. I distinctly remembered that I had been reading in Grandmother's parlor, so I knew this had to be some kind of aberration.

The voice was stronger here, but still unintelligible. I walked down the stairway and as I got closer to the dressing room, the voice grew louder, stronger, but the words were still unclear. I opened the door, stopped and at first could see no one. A mist formed in front of the make-up table and transformed into the figure of Irene. She did not look around as I walked in, but only continued to speak. She was quoting Shakespeare. This time it was Portia's speech from *The Merchant of Venice* — "The quality of mercy is not strain'd..." but she spoke in such a harsh, cold way. There was no softness, no mercy in her tone.

On the table before her was her diary, which she paged though as she spoke. She stopped her speech and started reading from the diary. The truly odd thing about her was that she was almost completely solid, only a slight haze around the edges. I was so surprised that my own speech caught in my throat. She looked up — not at me — but at my reflection in the mirror. Our positions had reversed since the last time I had seen her like this and the thought penetrated my senses that she was exchanging places with me. I shook with the horror of that idea...that I was about to lose my self.

At this moment, Gus silently padded into the room. His ears and his tail were up and he was alert. He paused by the door and looked up at Irene. The vision was completely surreal and I thought how strange that Gus was there in my dream.

Then, Irene began to speak to me.

"I can tell how you feel, Lillian, because I feel it. We are connected, you and I. I've tried so hard to allow you to see me and now you do—we are coming together. Through you, I live—because of you, I can exist. Teddy has tried to come between us each time, but not today. Today belongs to us, today sees the fulfillment of all I want."

Again, I thought as one does in dreams. *How odd*, I thought. *She wants something she cannot have. She is dead, after all, and I am the living one.* And then, I became conscious that all I had was my reflection in the mirror—I was traveling in my sleep again. At the same time, I was present in the dressing room and I could "see" my body in repose upon the sofa in Grandmother's parlor. Irene turned to me.

"It won't hurt at all. I just step into your body and you stay here. I was shortchanged. I want the rest of my life."

Just then, Gus jumped up onto the dressing table and onto her shoulder. He dug his claws into her and he clung onto her. Irene screamed in outrage and tried to throw him off. It gave me enough time to turn and run out of the room. I knew I had to be the first to get to my body. I knew I had to get back to the parlor and take possession first. If she took over, if she got there first, she would enter my body and I would indeed be lost.

Gus jumped down and he ran past me and I followed, moving as quickly as I could, Irene directly behind me. I could feel her coldness.

"Lillian, you'll never make it. I'm stronger, you've given me that strength, and you're the weak one now."

Suddenly, I found myself on the ceiling of Grandmother's parlor. I could see my body quite clearly—every fold in my dress, every wrinkle, but I couldn't feel my body. I couldn't feel the heat of the room or coldness of Irene's presence or even the pressure of my right ankle over my left. All I knew was I had to get back into my body and I had to do it *now*. Irene was so close, her presence was almost overpowering and she only pressed on. We both moved closer and closer and I willed myself into my body. I imagined all the familiar feelings of being in my body—the things I took for granted, the feel of my hair on the back of my neck, the feel of my hands as I rubbed them together, the pure pleasure of laughing out loud, how loved I felt when Mother embraced me...and suddenly, I woke up. I was back in my body.

My heart raced at an accelerated pace and a part of me relished the feel of that beat, appreciated the frantic pounding so dearly that I almost immediately started to calm down. At the same time, I could feel the chill in the air and knew Irene was there. I could feel her anger and frustration, and at that moment, knew I had to shut her out completely. I never again wanted to put myself into the position where I would lose the physical possession of my body. Irene would not, could not be allowed. In my mind, or it might have been from a great distance, I heard a howl of rage and frustration and knew Irene was not ready to give up.

I sat upright, stood up and hugged myself. It was so good to be back in my body. I appreciated everything about myself now and knew I had to work on controlling my "traveling" so that nothing like that would ever happen again.

I walked out of the parlor and into the foyer and looked at the grandfather clock. A mere quarter of an hour had passed since I lay on the sofa. Hardly any time at all. I knew for the rest of the day, I had to keep alert. I did not want to allow myself into the trap of drifting off again and feeling the lightness that precluded my travels. I knew then that I had to end my performance as Lady Macbeth and not risk the role even one more time. After dinner, I planned to tell Grandmother of my decision and we would draft a telegram to Mr. Daly together.

I didn't trust myself to go onstage again and I certainly did not trust what Irene would do next. I no longer cared who had killed her. I went into the kitchen to see if I could help Cook prepare dinner. I knew I had to become occupied in something physical and I had to do so quickly.

At dinner that night, I began to look at those around me with new eyes. Grandmother talked about a trip she wanted to take to New York and I joined her in what became a very animated discussion about the theater. I had to say I enjoyed every minute of it.

At around six that night, Thomas showed up at the front door with a telegram. He was slightly older than Bobby had been—around fifteen—and he didn't linger at the door, merely saying that this had been left for me at the theater and he brought it right over. He had other errands to run and so he departed quickly.

I opened the telegram and read that Mr. Daly had hired Clara Morris to play Lady Macbeth. She was an actress well-known for her portrayal of dramatic roles and a personal favorite of Mr. Daly. I wondered what he promised her in exchange for agreeing to come to Chicago, but I have to say an enormous feeling of relief flooded through my body. I was saved from communicating with Mr. Daly! My career was still possible. While my time as the female star of *Macbeth* was over, I no longer had to struggle with Irene. I would move on in my life, without her influence.

The note further said there would be a rehearsal that night, as Mr. Portman was anxious to get the changeover done as quickly as possible and not miss a performance. I was to be at the theater at 8:30 that evening, along with the rest of the cast who were in the Lady Macbeth scenes.

I changed my clothes and prepared to go to the theater. I wondered what would happen next in my career. I assumed I would go back to being a supernumerary, but perhaps they would want me to be an understudy to Lady Macbeth—or perhaps they wouldn't want me at all.

Mary would like that very much, I thought. What was I going to do about Mary? Would she be there tonight or would I never see her again? My mind was still working on that puzzle while sitting in Grandmother's coach on the way to the theater.

When I exited the coach, the wind that had blown all day had not abated in its intensity and it made things appear surreal. It whipped through my clothes and created whirlwinds of the leaves on the street. As I walked down the alley toward the stage door, I saw that it was already open, swinging back and forth on its hinges as the wind played with it. I walked in. Teddy was not behind his desk, but the gas lights were on.

It was very quiet. Once again, I appeared to be the first to arrive.

"Anyone else here?" I called out.

No answer. I walked onto the stage and over to where the reading table had been set up and chairs placed around it. Perhaps, there would be a read-through first. I set my gloves and purse on the table and began to walk around the stage. Something brushed against my leg and I almost jumped out of my skin. I looked down and there was Gus, his golden eyes fixed intently upon my face, as if he were trying to tell me something. I bent over and picked him up and held him close.

"Thank you," I whispered into his thick soft fur.

He had saved me from Irene and, as far as I was concerned, he was the best cat in the world. He purred loudly and rubbed his head against my cheek. I would have taken him home, but I knew that was not the life for him; like me, he wanted to be right where he was. I sat down on one of the chairs and began to scratch him behind his ears. He was in ecstasy and then, his head jerked up, his body tensed. He leapt out of my arms so quickly and with such force, that he left a long scratch on my left arm. I cried out in pain and stood up. He disappeared into the dim theater.

Blood began to seep from the scratch so I got out of the chair and took a step forward to get a handkerchief out of my purse. It was that movement that saved my life. At that same time, one of the set pieces flew straight up into the fly space of the theater and a very large sand bag crashed down and landed on the chair I had just vacated, reducing it to splinters.

I looked up just in time to see other bags falling toward me and knew I had to get off the stage now. There was no time to run right or left—it was all too far away. Heart racing, I ran straight for the front of the stage and leapt into the orchestra pit. I had no idea where I was going to land, but fortunately missed the music stands and landed on the conductor's platform.

What was going on? I looked back at the stage in wonder. Sand bags crashed onto the stage one after another. Someone had let loose the counter weight system on every piece of scenery that flew and now the stage was in chaos. Scenery fell over and flats hurtled through the darkness and collided with one another. Huge clouds of dust rose as they hit the floor. The noise was incredible. Had I stayed on stage, I would now be lying dead below some sandbag and buried beneath a pile of scenery from Act II.

My first thought was that somehow Irene was behind all this. I had closed off all my senses to her, establishing control, but now I tried to see if I could sense her presence. I released a little of my control, but there was nothing, so I pulled back in again. I never wanted to risk losing dominion of my mind and body ever again. But, I could sense that it was not Irene. What was happening was definitely of human, living origin. Dust flew everywhere, making it hard to see and breathe. I began to cough and I backed up, heading for the stairway that led out of the orchestra pit and into the house.

Just then, I heard a woman's scream. It was filled with frustration and rage and I was forcibly reminded of Irene, but I still could not sense her presence.

"Why don't you die?"

The carnage on the stage had ended and the dust was beginning to settle when I saw the lone figure of a tall and thin woman, completely dressed in black, standing off stage right. It was Beatrice O'Neill. She had put Irene's plaid shawl over her shoulder and pinned it in place with a piece of jewelry. She had re-strung the pearls, placed them around her own neck and they hung to her knees.

"Mrs. O'Neill," I gasped.

She turned at the sound of my voice and took a step toward me.

"Why don't you die?" she asked in a low voice. "You put your nose into everything. You had to interfere with things that did not concern you. I heard you asking questions. I saw the evidence of your search through Irene's possessions. You should never have been Lady Macbeth. You could never be what she was."

"Mrs. O'Neill, calm down...the others will be here soon–"

At that, she started to laugh.

"You are so stupid."

I had to admit, she had a point. I knew then, of course, that no one else was coming. I also knew Grandmother didn't expect me back for hours. Abruptly, I felt Irene's presence and I heard her laughter—an ugly, sarcastic laugh. I was on my own with Mrs. O'Neill. I knew now why I could not feel Irene's presence. She was not going to do anything to help me this time.

It was plain that Mrs. O'Neill heard nothing.

"I knew Irene kept a diary and I knew she was up to something. But, she would never tell me what—just that it was none of my business. One day, I followed her and saw her with Mr. Connelly. The way she acted with him—simpering and flattering—it was so unlike her! She was planning something, but I needed to know what. I searched and searched, but I could not find the diary. But you found it for me, didn't you? I knew you read it; you had to know what Irene was planning. But then Mary stole it."

I said nothing, just kept backing up toward the stairs to the house. Perhaps I could get away from her and out through the front of the theater.

"I knew you followed Mary and then, I thought, what if you just disappeared? No one would know what happened to you and no one would know Irene's story."

That gave me pause. I could not believe this woman could know what went on in the Underworld, pretend kindness to me and then leave me in that place.

"You knew I was there and you did nothing?"

"You did not matter to me."

And then, she cried out in pain.

"Only Irene, only Irene mattered!"

Her voice cut off sharply, as if she caught herself and suppressed that pain in some deep place and took a step toward me.

"Irene was going to marry him and just leave me—after all I had done for her!"

Then she moved toward me.

"You think you can take her place! You will never take her place!"

She looked straight at me, holding me in place with her gaze.

"I saw that you went through Irene's things. I saw that you pushed her possessions out of the way. I found the diary in the trunk where you meant to hide it."

Once again, I began to inch my way toward the stairs and into the auditorium.

"You got it back, didn't you? Now, it's mine."

She held up the small leather bound book.

She paused and in the silence, we could both hear the wind howl around the outside of the theater.

She took a step forward.

I made a run for the stairs, but she was too quick for me. She was there before I got to the top step and she pushed me back down. She had one of the battens from the counter weight system and was holding it in her hand, ready to strike me with it. I quickly backed away.

"It would be so easy to kill you now. I've done it before."

"Irene," I whispered.

"She was going to leave me," she howled. "I confronted her about Mr. Connelly and she laughed at me. I had been with her for twelve years, served her, did whatever she asked, saw to her every personal need—and this was how she was going to repay me! I knew all her secrets and I kept them. I loved her, but she was going to marry a wealthy man and leave me without a future, without any recompense for all I had done for her!"

She caressed the pearls that hung around her neck.

"It was so easy. I took care of her precious pearls. How many times had I seen her bow to an audience and throw them back over her head—always a crowd pleaser. That's how I got the idea. I knew her so well. I wanted her to die; I wanted her to die in a humiliating, public way. The afternoon of the opening, I restrung her pearls with wire. She put them on, as always, and she never suspected. That night, I stood in the wings and watched her final performance. No one ever pays any attention to me. I can get in and out of anywhere without being seen."

I understood now—dressed as she always was in black, she easily blended into the shadows. She could go just about anywhere backstage and not be seen. Everyone accepted her presence, but no one ever really looked at her.

Their focus would all be on their work during a performance—she would literally blend into the scenery.

"I had seen her perform Lady Macbeth so many times. I knew about the scenery change right after her last scene. I came in early that morning and screwed in a series of hooks into the flats, any of which could have caught the pearls. Only, I think someone saw me—"

"Bobby," I whispered.

"Before I had a chance to remove them, I overheard him asking one of the scene changers why someone would put hooks on the edge of the flats and what was the purpose of that? I had to eliminate him before he told someone it was me."

"How could you?" I cried

"I had to," she moaned.

"He was just a boy. He didn't know anything."

She screamed in pain.

"I didn't know that for sure! I had to be sure!"

She moaned again and began to sway.

"Now, you know. I have nothing left. Nothing to lose."

Suddenly, she turned back to me. There was a wildness in her expression difficult to describe.

She suddenly said, "You pretended to care for Bobby, but it was you all along. You wanted to take Irene's place."

I thought now she must be losing her mind.

"What are you talking about?"

"It's all there in Irene's diary. She wrote in it the last day she died."

"There was no entry that day," I said.

"Yes, there was."

She opened the diary and held it out to me. The writing looked remarkably like Irene's, but it was not hers. The entry described how I had threatened Irene unless she would give me the position of understudy. I had found out about her and Roger Plant, her life in the Underworld and I was going to blackmail her. Irene "feared" for her life. The whole idea was preposterous, but not to Beatrice O'Neill. In her mind, it all made sense.

"You die, I find this and give it to the police. You were the one that killed Bobby. Everything fits into place. I am the heroine who solved Irene Davenport's death. I am the one and Mr. Daly will find me a new position in gratitude for finding Irene's killer."

It was at that moment that I realized I had seen Beatrice before. She had appeared in the dream I had of Irene's leaving the Underworld. She was the one who was holding the baby, Mary, as Irene walked up the stairs.

"You raised Mary!"

That gave her pause. She was surprised and it seemed to bring her back to herself.

"Yes, I was responsible for her until she was six. I did that for Irene, too, so she could leave without looking back. But, by then, Irene was well-known, so I wrote to her. I told her I wanted out. We had been friends. I was there when Mary was born. I helped her. She agreed to give me a job, but I had to come to Philadelphia. I stole the money and I got out. When I got to Philadelphia, she tried to get out of our agreement. But, I knew everything about her past and where she came from; I knew who she was. I told her I would go straight to the newspapers. Actresses have such bad reputations anyway, but she had created a whole new identity for herself and I could destroy it. And so, she gave me the job she promised, but I became Irene's personal slave. I just exchanged one form of bondage for another. I didn't care. I loved her."

I could feel the pain Beatrice had gone through. She cried out, "But then, she was going to betray me. She was going to abandon me!"

A figure in white emerged from the darkness of stage right behind and beyond where Beatrice stood. My first thought was that an angel had come to save me, but I immediately shook that off as ridiculous. As the figure stepped forward, my eyes focused and I could see that it was Mary. She was dressed entirely in white and was more angelic than ever.

Her face was contorted in anger and hate. She pointed at Beatrice.

"You! It was you who left me there! Irene was never a mother to me, but you–"

She threw herself at Beatrice and the diary went flying onto the stage and came to rest upon a pile of debris.

Beatrice slapped Mary so hard that she went down to her knees and she turned and ran for the diary. Mary jumped up and pursued Beatrice, right on her heels. She rammed into her and they both went down, sending a cloud of dust rushing into the air. Mary got hold of the diary first.

"Give me that diary!" screamed Beatrice.

Mary attempted to crawl away from her, but it was difficult to get her balance among the refuse of the scenery. Beatrice pulled her back, ripping Mary's dress, which was now filthy from the dirt and dust.

I could hear Irene's laughter from somewhere in the upper regions of the roof of the theater. As the two struggled for the diary, they remained oblivious to the change in atmosphere on the stage. The air around me began to chill. I felt the hair on the back of my neck stand on end and goose bumps ran down my arms.

I ran up the stairs to the stage and over to them. I helped Mary up and pulled her away from Beatrice.

"Stop it you two—stop it! Irene is here now. She wants you Beatrice. We've got to get out of the theater!"

Beatrice now held the diary and I had to use all my strength to hold Mary back. I could tell Beatrice now thought I was the crazy one.

"Don't try to get out of this like you did in Roger's Barraks—making Ann believe some tale about a ghost. She was frantic," Beatrice shouted at me.

"Can't you feel it? Can't you feel the cold?" I yelled.

Mary stopped struggling. Our breaths came out and froze in the air. I knew she could feel Irene's presence. A shadow formed out of the clouds of dust and began to move toward us.

Beatrice paused.

"What do you mean?" she asked, beginning to shake.

A small wisp of smoke made its way down from the ceiling of the theater and curled and spun in front of us. The acrid smell of it filled my lungs and I coughed. It frightened me, but I thought somehow Irene had manufactured it.

"She's standing behind you right now."

I could tell Beatrice finally believed because she turned to look, then dropped the diary and screamed. Mary made a dive for it.

The wind howled, a strange light filled the theater and the smell of smoke became overpowering. At that very moment, we heard the windows in the lobby shatter in an explosion of glass and wood.

...when we hold rumour
From what we fear, yet know not what we fear,
But float upon a wild and violent sea
Each way and move.

Macbeth Act IV, Scene 2

~~~~~~

CHAPTER THIRTEEN

The explosion was horrific. Everything seemed to erupt at the same time in a cataclysmic blast of glass, wood and plaster. It was as if the end of the world had come. The doors leading into the auditorium disintegrated with the force of the onslaught and threw shards of glass and wood as far as the orchestra pit. Smoke poured in and began to cover everything in sight.

Mary had the diary in her hand and was trying to pull herself up off the floor. Beatrice stood frozen in the middle of the carnage on the stage and I saw Irene's apparition right behind her. She was clearly visible now and she moved toward Beatrice with the full focus of her will.

Smoke continued to pour in from the front of the theater. The whole building shook and it felt as if it were about to collapse. Bits of debris started to fall from the fly space and I looked up to see flames running along the wooden parts of the rigging. The roof was on fire. On the stage right side, a piece of flaming debris fell onto the deep velvet blue act curtain and it erupted into flames. The wreckage from the scenery that littered the stage began to smoke and then burn.

Stage right and the exit to the alley way were now blocked off by the fire. I ran toward the stairs leading to the orchestra pit and thought I could get to the stage left area through there. The fire had not reached that side of the stage yet. I knew I had to get out or I was going die here. I yelled for Mary and Beatrice.

Mary began to move towards me, but Beatrice stood upstage center as Irene whipped around her. Paralyzed by fear, Beatrice could not move. I could not tell if she could see me. Pieces of scenery, chairs, sandbags, rigging, everything began to lift off the floor and form into a vortex that swirled around Beatrice. It started slowly, but quickly gained in volume, momentum and height.

Mary was close to the swirling vortex and I screamed for her to get back. Her face was a mask of fear and I worked my way to her and attempted to pull her from the edge of the swirling mass. I managed to grab her arm, but then the two of us were blasted back toward the stage left wings by the force of the whirlwind. I fell on my right side with Mary next to me. She groaned.

"Mary, are you all right?" I yelled over the roar of the wind.

"I think so."

We were both filthy, our exposed skin covered in small cuts and scratches. The smoke was closing in on us, making breathing difficult and we both started to cough. We helped each other to stand.

"What'll we do? Can we get out the front?" Mary asked.

"It's completely destroyed."

We heard an unearthly scream and we turned toward Beatrice. She had been raised up into the swirling tornado and was being thrown about in it. As hot as it was in the theater, I could still feel Irene's coldness and her fury, as well as her satisfaction of having Beatrice at her mercy. Beatrice frantically called to us, but there was nothing either of us could do. Her body flew up at a tremendous rate and then was thrown down, hitting the stage floor with incredible force.

As the spinning vortex collapsed with her fall, another part of the roof crashed down upon her, pinning her to the stage. She was on her back, her broken body twisted in horrible contortion. Her eyes were open and her face was frozen in horror.

Mary and I watched in astonishment as two luminescent orbs of light appeared from among the carnage. The glow of the fire reflected in their centers and they began to circle one another and we heard a high-pitched, keening noise that reverberated through the air and our bodies. They flew faster and faster. They began to crash into each other and each time they met, a tremendous wail echoed through the theater. The hatred between Irene and Beatrice fueled the energy that made their spirits pursue one another even after death. The ugliness and darkness of it all was palpable.

The globes sped up to the point that they were just a blur and then, spiraled up and up toward the ceiling. As I watched them disappear through the gaping roof, the night sky looked as if it was on fire.

"Mary, we have to get out of here, now!"

She seemed to be frozen in place.

"Mary–"

"Alright, alright. How? We can't get out the front or the back."

We were surrounded by flames, and I realized the only way out was down. We couldn't get to the lower level of the theater where the dressing rooms and the load-in space was through the stairway off stage right. We would have to go down through the traps in the floor of the stage. I pulled her downstage and over to the trapdoor furthest from the flames on stage right. The wood was warm to the touch, but not hot.

Mary immediately understood what I was trying to do. She bent down and helped me with the trap door. We threw it back and stared down into a smoke-filled, black abyss. We looked at each other.

"It's our only chance." I said.

She nodded.

"I'll go first. Then, you'll have to jump down after me."

"Alright."

I sat down and dangled my feet through the opening. I held my breath and let myself drop down and landed on the floor beneath the stage. When I looked back up at Mary, all I could see was a shadowy, white figure. There was a dark haze below the stage, but no real smoke or fire that I could detect. I was dimly aware of where I was, due to the light of the fire, which shone through the cracks and seams of the stage floor from above.

"Hurry, Mary!"

For a split second, I thought she wasn't coming and the panic began to rise in my chest that I was all alone. Then, Mary's form suddenly appeared through the opening. I grabbed at her dress and she fell on top of me. We hit the floor with a thud. My head smarted from the impact, but other than that, I remained unhurt. We helped each other to stand and we took a breath, trying to get our bearings.

The haze made everything surreal and I could not get a sense of direction or where we were exactly, in relation to the loading doors and the exterior of the building. A shadow moved out from behind a pile of boxes and I saw a flash of golden eyes.

"Mary—look, it's Gus!"

He turned and waited for us, just on the edge of what we could see, then moved away as we approached. Gus led us down a corridor and then turned right. Above us, we could hear the creaking of the building as it began to disintegrate and the rigging as it fell and hit the stage floor. Then, we heard a noise like a gunshot and a rigging pipe come through the floor right behind us. It grazed the back of Mary's leg and she collapsed, throwing the diary into the darkness.

I ran back over to her and she moaned in pain.

"The diary—"

When I pulled back her dress, her right leg was a mass of blood.

"We don't have time—it's lost."

She looked at her leg and under the dirt on her face, she went pale.

"Lillian, help me."

I knew I couldn't leave her. I had no idea what to do. Her leg had to be bandaged—but with what? I looked at what was left of her white dress. I leaned over and ripped the hem out and started to wrap it around her leg. She cried out in pain.

"I'm sorry, I'm sorry, but I don't know what else to do."

She clenched her teeth and nodded.

"Can you stand?"

"I don't know."

I helped her up and when she attempted to put any weight on her leg, she yelped.

"You're going to have to use me as a crutch and we have to go now—do you understand me?"

She nodded. I put my arm around her shoulder and she did the same with me. Gus had circled back and he was meowing at us in an urgent way.

The volume of the noise around us had increased and I knew we had very little time—if any at all—to get out of the theater.

In a kind of bizarre three-legged race, Mary and I worked together and continued to follow Gus and he never let us stop—urging us on when we slowed down. We were near the dressing rooms and I knew the load-in dock was not far away. In front of us was the ramp leading up to the delivery doors and the street. Gus sat at the bottom of the ramp and looked at us.

I sat Mary down on a barrel and ran up the ramp ahead of me. We could hear the wind wailing through the street and we had no idea what was on the other side. I reached out and placed my hand against the wood of the huge door.

"It's not hot. I think we can get out this way."

I threw the bolt and tried to open the door, but the wind pushed against it with tremendous force. I looked around and found an ax and began hacking away at the door. A tremendous gust of wind grabbed the door and tore it off its hinges, throwing it back into the loading dock, just missing me. I looked back for Gus and just as I spotted him, he turned and ran back into the smoke filled darkness.

"Gus!" I yelled.

I turned to follow him, but Mary shouted at me to stop.

"Let him go. There is no time to go back! "

I went over to Mary, pulled her off the barrel and dragged her with me. We burst out of the back of the theater and onto Monroe Street. What met us there was a world gone mad.

...prophesying with accents terrible
Of dire combustion and confus'd events
New hatch'd to the woeful time.

Macbeth Act II, Scene 3

∞∞∞∞∞∞∞∞∞∞∞∞∞∞∞∞∞∞∞∞∞

CHAPTER FOURTEEN

The sky was lit up by the raging fire shooting out from the burning buildings that lined the street and made it as bright as day. Above us, sparks and flying debris shot from one building to the next as the incredible force of the wind created a storm of fire and spread the conflagration at a fantastic pace. The roar of that wind was incredible—I not only heard it, but felt it throughout my body and it struck a deep fear into my heart. I could only stand with Mary and stare. How were we ever going to survive this?

The hour was very late, but the street was jammed with mobs of people from every possible walk of life who were making their way to the Chicago River. We had escaped death in the theater, only to find ourselves in the middle of hell.

As we stood there, a man separated himself from the crowd and came over to us.

"Mary? Lillian?"

I looked up at his face, but it was Mary who recognized him first.

"Jack! Oh, Jack!"

"What are you doing here?"

She started to explain. "We were in the theater…"

"You've got to get out of here now."

I finally found my voice.

"Mary is hurt. It's her leg, she can't walk. You'll have to help me."

He kneeled down in front of Mary to examine her leg and then, he looked back up at me. His eyes were wide and I could tell he was shocked and worried by what he saw.

"We can't stay here or we'll be caught in the fire," was all he said.

He lifted Mary up in his arms and began to move down the street as quickly as he could. I followed along behind as we merged into the river of those fleeing the blaze.

He turned to me and said, "When I got to Roger's Barracks, it was gone."

For a minute, that cheered me considerably. I was thrilled that that horrible place had been blasted to hell. But then, I couldn't help but think of all the people that were there and wondered if they had gotten out. A part of me didn't really care what happened to Sally or Ann, or even Roger Plant, but I did wonder what would become of the little girls.

"Lillian, keep up!"

I realized he had gone on ahead of me and if I didn't catch up, I would be lost in the mob of people who were trying to escape the fire. Some dragged trunks after them, others were laden with their possessions, buggies, carts, coaches, and all kinds of conveyances clogged the streets making it difficult to maneuver. If their baggage got too heavy, or the flames too close, they merely dropped whatever they were carrying and moved on. The sidewalks became impassable, piled high with discarded leavings.

Jack was insistent that we move west and cross the river.

A Fire Department steamer came by us, the driver urging his team through the mass of humanity. He called to us.

"The Madison Bridge is gone—you can try Randolph, but that might be in flames too by now. Try getting to the North side."

And he and the team were gone as quickly as they came, the mass parting to make way for them.

Suddenly, I knew we had to get to Grandmother's. Surely, the fire hadn't reached the north side and we would be safe there.

"Jack, let's go north. We can get to my grandmother's. We can get help for Mary and we'll be alright."

"It will take us all night to get there at this rate! No, let's get out of this entirely. If we can make it across the river, we can get onto the prairie."

"But, what if that catches fire? We'll be dead before we know it!"

We stopped where we were standing. As he held Mary in his arms, the two of us argued about what we were going to go next. The surge of humanity just went around us. I could only think of Grandmother and what a haven her home was for me. I knew if I could just get there, I would be safe.

"I want to go to Grandmother's. I want to make sure she's all right. The fire can't jump the river to the north."

I could tell he was torn by the decision of which way to go. Flames were flying a hundred feet over our heads, leaping from rooftop to rooftop; the wind was screaming and throwing debris from the remains of the buildings that had surrendered to the fire.

As we stood in the middle of the street, a horse and buggy came up behind us. The man driving it yelled at us.

"Get the hell out of the way!"

We looked up.

A woman was sitting next to him, holding a tightly wrapped baby in her arms.

Jack immediately ran over to him.

"Do you have space for my wife? Can you help us?"

The baby made a whimpering noise and the woman rocked it.

"There's no room," the man said.

"Please. She's hurt her leg and can't walk."

The woman looked down at the blood on Mary's dress and then, at her husband.

"Jonathan, we can squeeze her in next to me."

Without permission, Jack lifted Mary into the buggy next to the woman, who immediately moved over.

"Jack?" Mark looked scared.

"Don't worry, Mary, I'll find my way—you just be safe."

All Mary said was, "Stay with Lillian. She needs your help."

The man shook his head, slapped the reins and they were off.

Mary leaned out and looked back at Jack and waved.

"I'll find you, Mary," Jack called.

"I know you will, Jack. I'll count on it."

And the buggy disappeared into the crowd and was completely lost from sight.

I stood there in the street watching him as he stared after the buggy long after it was gone, swallowed into the mass of people. A different sort of pain coursed through my body and I quickly realized it was jealousy. He obviously loved her. Did she deserve him or his love? Every fiber in my body screamed no! But, I also didn't know if they were ever going to see one another again. I had no idea if any of us were going to make it out of this conflagration alive.

"Jack…"

"Alright, alright. Let's just move."

He took off down the street and I had to run to catch up with him. The sound and fury of the wind and flames as the fire moved onward were incredible. Buildings were falling behind us and we could hear the echo of their collapse. Glass exploded out of store windows. In the crowd, women and children cried and screamed in fear and desperation. A thick dust rose up, pushed by the wind, making visibility difficult and stinging our faces.

We continued on, the fire at our backs. We saw people breaking widows on stores not yet consumed by the fire, dragging out merchandise and then, abandoning it, finding it too much to bear. They dropped what they could not easily carry. The streets were filled with discarded objects. Firebrands landed on many of these piles and started new fires.

It was so hot and I was so thirty. We worked our way up Dearborn, and when we got to the bridge, found we could not get through and had to turn back and make our way over to Clark Street. We were hoping we could cross there and get over to the north side of the Chicago River.

We joined the crowd that seemed to have the same idea and looked up to see flaming wreckage floating in the wind over our heads. It quickly landed on the other side of the river, setting buildings ablaze. I couldn't believe it. The fire had crossed the river. We couldn't go back; we could only press on.

We joined the river of people that streamed onto Randolph Street to cross there. The street was solid with men, women and children, their possessions, animals, and wagons. Many belongings were abandoned and we had to make our way through everything from discarded oil paintings, books, and musical instruments to toys and bedding. I worried that I would trip and fall over some useless possession and be trampled to death. People jammed together shoulder to shoulder and I had to trot to keep up with Jack. I was afraid I would lose him among the masses and then I would truly be alone. He grabbed my hand, pushed people out of the way and created a path for us. Following closely, the firestorm raging above us, we managed to cross the bridge.

Just across the river, we only had a few blocks to go to get to Grandmother's. A horse, wild-eyed, out of control and dragging the remnants of a buggy behind it, came charging through the crowd. People scattered and Jack pushed me out of the way and onto the side of the street where I fell onto a pile of someone's belongings. The side of the buggy clipped his shoulder and threw him onto the sidewalk near me. I pulled myself up and ran over to him. There was a huge gash on his head and blood streamed down the side of his face. He was unconscious.

"Jack, Jack!" I cried.

There was no response.

I sat next to him, put my arms around him and rocked him in the midst of all the chaos and destruction taking place around us. I didn't know what to do. I would not leave him.

"You have to wake up, Jack, I can't do this by myself. Please wake up."

He moaned and I was never so glad to hear such a sound in my life.

And then, sparks started to fall around us and several landed on the sleeve of my dress, quickly caught fire and burned through the fabric. I screamed in pain and that brought Jack to full attention.

My dress was on fire and Jack ripped off his jacket and wrapped it around me, putting out the flames. I was in agony. My arm throbbed and the pain was incredible. Jack looked at me helplessly.

"We have to move, Lillian."

I looked at him blankly.

"We have to go," he urged.

It was too much. I just wanted to stay there and die. Let the smoke and the dust and the fire roll over me and leave nothing behind.

"Get up, come on, Lillian. Now."

He practically lifted me off the curb and dragged me down the street. We continued that way until we got to Ohio Street. Grandmother's house was just a few blocks away. We moved against the tide of people that were heading for the Lake. A few of the homes we passed were smoking and some of the homeowners were doing their best to keep the fire at bay by taking down fences and removing leaves. A man on the roof of one house we passed was placing carpets over the shingles and wetting them down. I was reminded of how thirsty I was.

We finally arrived at Grandmother's to find her standing on her front porch, directing her coachman as he loaded the coach with some of her more prized possessions. She had at least three dresses on and what looked like all her jewelry. I was never so glad to see her in my life. She looked up and saw me and at that moment, time stopped.

"Rosemary," she cried and ran down the steps to me. "I didn't know what to think had happened to you!"

She wrapped her arms round me and I cried in agony.

"What's the matter? What is it?"

Jack spoke up and said, "Her arm was burned."

"Oh, my poor girl. Let's get that seen to right away."

She took us in the house and found some bandages and ointment. She carefully removed Jack's coat and looked at my arm. Grandmother is a truly amazing woman; she didn't flinch once when she looked at the burned flesh. I wanted to pass out, but didn't. In a very short time and as carefully as possible, she cleaned the wound and bandaged it. She got Jack something to drink and then, she gave me some water. Nothing had ever tasted so good.

"We filled as many jugs as I could find with water. They are packed and ready to go."

"Go? Where are you going?" I asked, "Are you going away?"

"Yes, we're all leaving, dear. The fire is headed this way. We have to get to the lake."

"What about Father and Mother and the boys?" I asked. "Have you heard from them? Are they safe?"

"Your father was here two hours ago—he went to see if he could find you. He told me they planned to go to Lincoln Park."

Above us, the wind continued to cry and throw sparks and flames. Several of them hit the roof of the house next door and it immediately started to burn.

"Ma'am, I think we should go, as well," Jack said.

Grandmother led us outside. The coach was full and Grandmother had planned to sit next to her coachman, but she would not allow me to walk. She took a few extra minutes to decide what really could be left behind and instructed him to pile it just inside the gate. That made enough room for me and I was helped into the coach, where I sat on top of a trunk that held the good china and crystal.

Jack turned to me and said, "I need to go find Mary."

I begged him to stay with us until we were safely at Lincoln Park and he reluctantly agreed and started walking beside the coach.

We drove into a nightmare. The fire still lit up the sky, but there was now a dusty haze clouding the air. I just sat in the coach and let the back and forth swaying of the carriage release all thoughts from my mind. I wanted to feel as if I were in another place and time entirely.

The sun came up—a very weak light in the rust-covered sky and still, the fire continued. In an amazingly short amount of time, we were at Lincoln Park. The southern edge of the park, until recently, had been a cemetery. The graves had been removed and divided up into Graceland, Oakwood, and Rosehill cemeteries. The last cemetery was where Irene's body had been laid to rest. The park was now crowded with people of every age and social status and all was in chaos and confusion. There were so many people and they all looked completely lost.

In this surreal world, among the abandoned headstones, we sought refuge in the early morning hours of Monday, October ninth. We could still tell from the wind and the smoke and flames in the sky that the fire raged on and that it had a strong hold on the north side. The coachman helped Grandmother down and Jack got me out of the coach.

Grandmother checked my arm before taking me over to an abandoned mausoleum and sat me down on a stone bench. She put her shawl around me and told me to rest. Then, she told me that Jack was leaving. I looked up at him in surprise.

"What? No! You can't leave us!"

Grandmother interrupted me.

"I've asked Jack if he would be willing to try and find out what happened to the rest of our family and he has agreed."

I was so weak, I didn't have the strength to argue. I just knew I didn't want him to leave me.

"Jack, you don't have to do this."

Grandmother interrupted me.

"Neither of us can go and I sent my coachman back to see if he can bring another load. There is no one else."

At that, Jack spoke up, "Lillian, I promised your grandmother I'd find them. After that, I have to find Mary."

Oh. Mary, yes, of course, he would want to know where she was and if she was all right. All I could say was "Take care of yourself, then."

He smiled at that, making funny creases in his dirt-streaked face.

"I always do."

He turned and walked away, quickly merging in with the crowd and was gone. I wondered if I would ever see him again. At that particular moment, I felt deeply sorry for myself. What was to happen to me? I was in pain, my arm would be scarred—I did not know if I would ever be able to use it again—and my family was gone. I had been so stupid. My theatrical career was over. What would I do with the rest of my life? Who would ever love me? Who wanted me? It was too much to bear and I began to cry.

Grandmother came over and sat down next to me and gave a deep, exhausted sigh. She put her arm around my good side and drew me close. I cried until I was completely drained of tears.

When I looked up, I saw that Grandmother had fallen asleep. I took a close look at her and realized how much older she was than I had previously thought. I couldn't imagine the toll that this whole experience had taken on her. Her home was probably gone now. It was the home where she came as a bride, had borne six children, and raised them to maturity.

I whispered. "I'm sorry about your house, Grandmother."

Her eyes opened and she gave me a worried look for a moment. Then she relaxed.

"Rosemary, it's just a house. It can be re-built."

That comforted me. Perhaps she was right. A house can be re-built; perhaps a life can be re-built, as well. I leaned back against the stone wall of the small building and closed my eyes. I must have drifted off because I was awakened much later by a group of people singing "Abide With Me":

> Abide with me; fast falls the eventide;
> The darkness deepens;
> Lord, with me abide;
> When other helpers fail and comforts flee,
> Help of the helpless, oh, abide with me.

Other voices picked up the song and, for a moment, it was as if time stood still and all that existed in that moment were those voices, joined together in that song.

The day wore on and it seemed as if a decision about whether or not we were all going to survive would be out of our control. The fire was immediately to the west of us and many people got close to the lakeshore, and even into the water. Many had left their belongings on the western edge of the park and much of it caught fire and was blazing, making people pull back towards the water.

That long day, we sat there and I worried about my family.

"Do you think they are alright?" I asked Grandmother

"Of course. Your father will see to it."

"How do you know?"

"Your father is the most capable man I know. Actually, the two of you are very much alike. Look where you are, how far you've come."

"I don't think we are alike at all," I said.

"Nonsense. Did you know your father wanted to be a writer? He was very talented, actually."

For the second time in a few short weeks, I found myself speechless.

"It's true. His father wouldn't let him. Told him he had to be responsible. I argued with your grandfather about it a great deal, but he was adamant. That must have been going through your father's mind when he forbade you to work in the theater. He had accepted the life his father wanted for him and made a success, and he believes that you can do the same. Rosemary, your father loves you. He is merely doing the best he knows how for you. You must learn to forgive him for that and accept his love."

I was quiet for a very long time, after that. All the noise receded into the background as I thought about her words and my family—Mother, Father, John William, and Francis—and I wondered if I would ever see them again. There were so many people here. How would Jack ever find them? If he did find them, would we ever be reconciled? What if I died here and we never had the opportunity? What if they were already dead? That was too painful to consider and I deliberately turned my thoughts to Irene and Beatrice. I wondered if their spirits would ever be at peace because they could not forgive one another.

Would they continue to pursue and hate each other in the afterlife of the Beyond?

My desire for a theatrical life seemed so small at this moment. It meant that I had estranged myself from my family and, if we were to meet God, would we receive His forgiveness, as well, for the pain we had caused each other?

I vowed that if I survived I would somehow make peace with them. I would not allow my life to continue without asking for forgiveness and forgiving them for our disagreements. I began to think of my actions in a new light and I knew I had to forgive myself, as well. I had to forgive myself for wanting what I wanted and letting myself have it, regardless of other's feelings. In that moment, I felt something loosen in my very being. I realized I was taking a new direction in my life, that I had grown up and had gained perspective that was unimaginable in my previous seventeen years. I knew my life truly would never be the same again.

I stood up and looked around and realized all the people around me had nothing left except what they had with them or on their backs. Either that was enough or it would never be enough.

The day wore on into night and still, the fire burned. And then, at about eleven o'clock that night, it began to rain.

Let us seek out some desolate shade, and there
Weep our sad bosoms empty.

Macbeth Act IV, Scene 3

~~~~~~

CHAPTER FIFTEEN

It was the rain that saved us. We stood in the old cemetery by the lakefront and looked up to the sky and wept as the rain fell. We were saved. The fire had reached the very edge of where we stood and backed us up to the shore of Lake Michigan. It had ignited the piles of abandoned belongings of the thousands who had surrounded us and we watched as the rain extinguished the flames. Smoke began to float in wisps of dark gray clouds across the debris. I stood there, filthy, my clothes scorched and pocked by burn holes. I was exhausted, in pain and wet, but I didn't care. I knew it was over.

Thomas Luck, the oldest son of Amelia Luck and one of Grandmother's dearest friends, found us in Lincoln Park later that day and took us away to his home on the north side in an area that had not burned. He had gotten word from Father, who had been located by Jack. On the way, I sat in his buggy and looked out on a landscape that I could never have imagined. The streets were lined with smoking refuse. Homes were completely destroyed or just shadow structures of their former selves. There were few people on the street, but the ones I saw looked dazed and lost.

Most noticeable was the lack of noise. Where Sunday night had been filled with the sound and fury of the fire and the screams of people out on the streets, and Monday had been filled with the noise of prayer and the singing of hymns, today was just eerily quiet. When we arrived, Amelia took us in, fed us and saw to my arm. That night, I went to sleep on an actual bed and was completely grateful for the experience.

The next day, feeling refreshed and much better from the sleep, food and good care, the only thing I wanted to do was see my family. I convinced Grandmother I had to go. She was still exhausted. The whole experience had drained her considerable reserves. She looked older than I had ever seen her. I promised her I would find out as much as I could and bring her back word. Mr. Luck agreed to drive me to our house. I had to know if it was still standing and if my family was there. Of course, they had no way of knowing if Mr. Luck had actually found us, what had happened to us, or even if we were alive.

We arrived at Ohio Street at eleven that morning. We passed Grandmother's house and all that was left standing was the front porch and one pillar. Our street was almost completely unrecognizable. There was no greenery, no sidewalks, and almost every building was gone. Later, I discovered that only two houses on the entire north side survived the fire. One of which was Mr. Manlon Ogden's house, just several blocks south on Lafayette Place facing Washington Park. Mr. Ogden was the brother of the first mayor of Chicago and he had been able to save his home through the help of many neighbors who had taken refuge there and the fact that wind had shifted at just the right time. I later visited it and saw the large mansion completely surrounded by blackened trees and smoldering wreckage, but the home was intact.

When I got to our house, I wanted to cry. My home was a mere shell of itself. All that remained was a corner of the house and the open, glassless window of my bedroom on the second floor. No one was around. No other buildings were left. I felt incredibly empty and alone, but suddenly, I saw a figure come from behind the remaining façade. It was Father.

I jumped out of the buggy and ran toward him, calling his name.

"Rosemary?"

He said my name as if he had never heard it before, as if he never expected to see me again.

"It's me, Father."

My usually immaculate father, who had never appeared in anything less than his banker's dress suit, wore dirty work clothes and had his sleeves rolled up to his elbows. His face was covered by the gritty dust and his eyebrows and mustache were singed.

A light came into his eyes and he ran toward me, caught me and threw his arms around me. He hugged me completely, fully and so thoroughly, in a way I hadn't felt since I was a small child.

"Thank God you're all right."

"What about Mother and the boys?"

"They're fine. They are at your Uncle Charles' house on the west side. How is—"

"Grandmother is fine. We are at the Lucks'."

He hugged me again and said, "Nothing else matters, Rosemary. You're all right, we all survived."

"The house—"

"It's just a house. It doesn't matter, it isn't important."

I looked up at him, at those eyes so like my own and saw that there were tears in his eyes.

"I'm so sorry, Father," I whispered, "but please don't make me give up my family for what I love. Don't make me split myself in two over this."

There was a long pause and I understood at that moment that it was because he could not bring himself to speak. He merely rocked me in his arms.

"Grandmother told me you wanted to be a writer," I said.

Finally, he said, "That was a long time ago."

"I'm so sorry, Father."

"I'm sorry, too, Rosemary."

In that moment, relief poured through my body. I hadn't realized the burden I carried. Now, I knew he truly forgave me. He loved me and I felt his love and his protection standing in the wreckage of our family home more than I had at any other time in my life.

And then, I knew. The disagreement that had separated us no longer mattered. It was the love that we had for each other that was important. The fire had taken every material possession from us, but we were alive. We had each other and we were all safe.

I asked him about Jack and he said that he had shown up at the house late in the afternoon on Monday and that he had helped to get the family out and up to the west side. Then, he had disappeared. Father had no idea where he went or what happened to him.

I would not believe that Jack was dead. He had saved my life and I had saved his. It was a bond that tied us together. He would find Mary or he would not find her, but I knew in the deepest part of my heart that someday we would meet again.

Chicago was shattered. Over three-hundred people lost their lives and one-hundred thousand were homeless. Every public building was destroyed and the theater district was hit hardest of all. Crosby's Opera House, where Irene's funeral service had been held and which was due to reopen on the ninth of October, fell to the flames. The Grand Theater also was gone and with it, Gus, as well as the McVickers, Falwell Hall, and many more. The Chicago Courthouse, which had filled an entire city block, was a crumpled mass of wreckage, along with the magnificent Sherman House and the despicable Conley's Patch—it was all gone. An astronomical two-hundred million dollars in damage was done—and much of it never recovered.

As you know, dear Agnes, our home, our city, is known as the "Gem of the Prairie" for good reason. The last house on the north side burned on Tuesday morning and on Tuesday afternoon the first load of lumber arrived at the mouth of the Chicago River to assist in rebuilding the city. In a strange turn of events, that lumber belonged to Mr. Samuel Connelly and he created another fortune in the rebuilding of Chicago. Had Irene married him, she would have been rich beyond her imagination. I wonder if she would ever have felt safe.

Chicago would rebuild faster than anyone could have ever imagined. Within three years, the city would once again take its place as one of the leading cities of our country.

The burn on my arm did eventually heal, but it left an ugly scar. Now you know why I have never been able to wear a short sleeved dress unless it was formal and I had long gloves to go with it. It is a continual reminder of my theatrical beginning and my home city.

However, I want you to know that in 1871, my life in the theater was not over. It was just beginning. In fact, all that I learned from my experience in *Macbeth* and with Irene has served me well these past eighty years. However, I have never appeared in another production of that play. It has been a matter of my choice. It is too closely associated for me with Irene Davenport and how I almost lost my very soul.

You should know that Grandmother continued to be the rock of my life until her death, and while my parents never approved of my career, they became reconciled to it. I was allowed to reunite with my brothers, who became my biggest supporters, often encouraging me at very low points in my life and always attending performances of plays whenever I appeared in Chicago.

And so I end this part of the memoir here. I like to think of this first story as the curtain warmer to a much more adventurous first act. That experience was a prelude to many more acts which I hope to share with you. It is my fondest desire that it has not bored you too much.

Lillian Nolan
Lake Forest
September 1951

ACKNOWLEDGMENTS

It was a privilege to practice my passion for theater by teaching on the college level for ten years. I taught selected courses, directed various plays, and ran the front of house operations for a vibrant performing arts department. I wish to thank my colleagues and students during that time who were a source of inspiration and so instrumental in teaching me what I needed to know.

It is with great appreciation that I acknowledge the support of my husband Jay, my daughter Mai Lan, and my sister, Jean during the writing process. I also wish to thank my fellow Alchemists, Laura Cooke, Sue Peters, Marguerite Rooney, Kathleen Ryan, and Deb Samuel for their unconditional support.

A number of people were instrumental in reading (and re-reading) drafts of the book. I am thankful for the generosity of time and constructive criticism of Kathleen

Smith, Tricia Molloy, Kathleen Schoenblum, Paula Keenan, and Jean McCormick.

My past and present writing partners, Park Borchert, Charlie Nooney, Mona Lyden Moore, and Kathleen Smith gave me enthusiastic support in my own writing endeavors.

Many thanks to Jessica Parker, Caroline Donahue, and Ellina Dent at BookLogix for their time and talent. In particular, I would like to thank Ahmad Meradji for running a fiction contest in which I was privileged to be the 2012 winner.

If one can thank a city, then I am grateful to the city of Chicago—the birthplace of both my father and myself and the inspiration for *Death Takes Center Stage*. It is a dynamic city, alive with theater. As Brian Dennehy wrote in the Foreword to Richard Christiansen's wonderful book, *A Theater of Our Own: A History and a Memoir of 1,001 Nights in Chicago*:

> When young people ask me how they can 'break into' this business, and the phrase 'break in' is all too appropriate, I always tell them to go to Chicago. Besides being a great place to live, there is a lot of theater going on, and if you can't get a job, you can always start your own theater. Everyone else does.

Good advice for writing as well.

~~~~~~~~~~~~~~~~~~~~~~~~~~~~~~~~~~~~~~~

About the Author

Elizabeth Ireland is a former associate professor of theater. She was a quarter-finalist and a semi-finalist for the *Don and Gee Nicholl Fellowship* in screenwriting sponsored by AMPAS. Her nonfiction work, *Women of Vision: Ordinary Women, Extraordinary Lives*, was published in 2008. Her work has also been published in a collection of paranormal short stories, *Paramourtal: Tales of Undying Love and Loving the Undead*. She lives in metro Atlanta with her ever-patient husband, an amazing teen-aged daughter, and two quirky dachshunds.

Learn about her upcoming work and the next installment in the Backstage Mystery series at:

www.ElizabethIreland.net
www.BackstageMystery.com